# Sherlock Holmes – The Baker Street Case-Files

## Another collection of previously unknown cases from the extraordinary career of Mr Sherlock Holmes

Mark Mower

Paperback ISBN  978-1-78705-120-1
ePub ISBN  978-1-78705-121-8
PDF ISBN  978-1-78705-122-5

Published in the UK by MX Publishing
335 Princess Park Manor, Royal Drive,
London, N11 3GX
www.mxpublishing.co.uk
Cover design by Brian Belanger
www.belangerbooks.com and www.redbubble.com/people/zhahadun

# Contents

*Preface*                                        4

1.  The Case of the Rondel Dagger             6

2.  The Melancholy Methodist                 45

3.  The Manila Envelope                       61

4.  The Radicant Munificent Society          76

5.  The Strange Missive of
    Germaine Wilkes                          104

6.  A Case of Poetic Injustice              117

7.  The Mile End Mynah Bird                 141

*About the Author*                          173

*Copyright Information*                     174

# Preface

Following the extraordinary success of the earlier volume, *A Farewell to Baker Street*, it was suggested to me that I should gather together another collection of previously unknown Holmes and Watson cases that could excite the interests of readers across the globe. This is my response to that challenge – *The Baker Street Case-Files*.

You will recognise that I have had to wait a good seven years in publishing this second volume. The nature of the recent global conflict almost scuppered the endeavour. But I was not to be put off! In these difficult times I believe we need to continue to demonstrate conviction, veracity and stoicism – qualities which Holmes and Watson displayed time and time again. I refused, therefore, to give up on the venture.

The stories I have chosen shed more light on the remarkable talents of Mr Sherlock Holmes. The first in the collection, *The Case of the Rondel Dagger*, occurred before my uncle was even known to the great detective. *The Mile End Mynah Bird* is a fascinating tale set in the period beyond The Great War when both men appear reluctant to retire. From the plotting of *The Radicant Munificent Society* to the hidden message of *The Manila Envelope*, there is much to entertain and enthral us.

There is still some way to go in exhausting the collection of forty-odd stories that I inherited from my uncle in 1939. We may yet see a third or even a fourth volume of tales – that very much depends on all of you, dear readers. For I am loath to set the printing presses to work unless this present book is favourably received. Time will tell.

As before, my sincere hope is that I have contributed in some small part to the lasting memory of these two extraordinary men. Once again, 'The game is afoot!'

Christopher Henry Watson, MD

Bexley Heath, Kent – 25th November 1946

# 1. The Case of the Rondel Dagger

*London, 5ᵗʰ March 1880 - it is unlikely that you will have heard of me prior to this, my first published narrative. For the past eight years I have worked as a research fellow at the British Museum in Bloomsbury, having graduated from Sidney Sussex College in Cambridge some years earlier with a First in Classics. While my choice of career has been rewarding and engaging to a point, it has not placed me at the forefront of academia in the way that I might have hoped for when I first left university in that long hot summer of 1865, a fresh-faced youth aching with ambition. And to the very great disappointment of my family, it has often been observed that I have failed to live up to their considerable expectations of me. As such, I would be very surprised to learn that anyone, of any particular standing, was already familiar with the name Charles Stewart Mickleburgh. And yet, with the events I am about to relate, I have every confidence that this will change rapidly – my story emanating from a chance encounter earlier this year with an extraordinary young man by the name of Sherlock Holmes.*

The adventure began on a snowy and bitterly cold morning in late January. I was the first to arrive at work that day, my rented house in Montague Street being but a five minute walk away from the annex of the museum in which I work. Being one of the more senior fellows, I am trusted with my own key and was about to use it to unlock the side door of the building when I halted abruptly. I could hear someone approaching from behind, their crunching footfall on the virgin snow ringing out audibly across the quadrangle. In the half-light of the early dawn I turned quickly and saw a tall, thin-faced man in a long, dark Ulster jacket and top hat striding towards me, a silver-topped cane swinging freely in his left hand. As he came to a halt, a thin smile radiated across his pale face and a gloved right hand was extended towards me. His look was one of evident intent; his bright, penetrating eyes and aquiline nose giving him an eager, hawk-like countenance and the rich timbre of his clear, clipped voice adding to the evident gravitas of his stature. I shook his hand, briefly, but courteously, as he spoke.

"Forgive me, Mr Mickleburgh. I can see that I have startled you. I grant you that it is indeed an odd hour to make your acquaintance, but do not, at present, have the luxury of time. I am currently engaged in a pressing matter, of international significance, and believe that you have some knowledge which might assist me. I had sought to call on you at home, for I reside only a few doors from you, but your early start had the better of me. As I set out along the icy and treacherous pavement of Montague Street, I could already see you heading off around the corner towards the museum. My only course of action was to follow you."

"Indeed, sir," I replied, desperately trying to process all that he had said, bewildered as to how he should know my name and speculating wildly on the nature of the international affair he had alluded to. "But you clearly have the upper hand, since you seem to know so much about me and yet I have no idea who you are."

The fellow chuckled at my retort and the radiant smile returned once more. "Etiquette has never been one of my strong suits, Mr Mickleburgh. Once again, you must forgive this forthright approach. My name is Sherlock Holmes and I am a chemist and detective of sorts. I have been asked to investigate a delicate incident involving a foreign diplomat. I understand that you are the British Museum's resident expert on ancient weapons, so it is to you that I naturally defer. I have an excellent working knowledge of modern firearms, knives, garrottes, poisons and other killing paraphernalia, but I would not profess to know a great deal about the weaponry of the middle ages."

He paused at that point as if seeking some sort of confirmation from me. I responded accordingly. "Well yes, I am something of an expert in that field, although my academic role extends more widely, to all aspects of criminal justice in the medieval period. I would be more than willing to help you, but could I suggest that we step inside, out of the cold, and resume this conversation over a hot beverage?"

"An excellent idea", said Holmes, stamping his feet and doing his best to dislodge as much of the snow that was clinging to his ankle boots as he could. I followed his lead and then unlocked the door. Having led my visitor down through a maze of corridors to the small windowless office I occupied at the rear of the annex, I beckoned for Holmes to take a seat close to the coal fire which had already been lit by one of the museum's night porters. Within ten minutes our hands were cupped around two hot cups of steaming tea I had prepared using a small black kettle hung within the open fire grate.

Our renewed conversation proved to be both absorbing and enlightening. Holmes was fascinated by the rare collection of leather-bound books I had assembled on crime and punishment in the Tudor period and which adorned every inch of shelf space within my cramped quarters. He also marvelled at the small display of pole cleavers which sat in one corner, as I explained the differences between the voulge, spetum, sovnya, glaive and bardiche weapons which he handled with enthusiasm. It was then that he turned to the nature of his enquiry, removing carefully from an inside pouch of his long jacket a heavily wrapped package, which he then unfurled before me. Inside, lay, what I instantly recognised as a rondel dagger, some eight or nine inches in length.

"Mr Mickleburgh. Since leaving behind my university studies, I have pursued a financially precarious vocation as an independent investigator; what I alone refer to as a *consulting detective*. And while I maintain good contacts with the official metropolitan force, and have occasionally been asked to assist Scotland Yard on some of its more obscure investigations, I operate autonomously - outside of any official jurisdiction - and choose carefully each and every client that I work for. This approach does not always endear me to those who seek my help, but I have a growing reputation as a man who can solve any manner of crime, riddle, puzzle or conundrum. I make it my business to observe things that others overlook and to solve every case presented to me on the basis of clear science and rational deduction. But I cannot operate without appropriate data and, when my own knowledge is found wanting, I recognise the absolute necessity of seeking out others with expertise." He paused and took a small sip from his tea, maintaining his intense stare, before continuing.

"I recently undertook a short and successful assignment for Lord Haverstock. As you may know, he is a trustee of the British Museum. When I asked him yesterday evening if he knew of an expert in medieval weaponry, it was your name that he first suggested. And when I learned later that you resided on Montague Street, it seemed as if you were, all ways round, the perfect man to consult. So, anything you can now tell me about the item in your lap would be very much appreciated."

A mixture of thoughts and emotions flooded through me - surprise that Lord Haverstock, whom I had met but twice in my career, should remember me; pride that my academic reputation actually meant something to someone; and humility that this clearly able and articulate young man should seek my help. I was determined to help him in any way that I could.

"Mr Holmes, you will recognise of course, that this is a replica weapon. Only a few original examples, from the fourteenth and fifteenth centuries, are known to exist. It is called a *rondel dagger*, the word 'rondel' meaning circular or round, and denoting its octagonal hand guard and the spherical pommel at the end of the grip. This weapon is well under a foot long; an original dagger would have been anywhere between twelve and twenty inches in length. The blade is made of steel and set within a very ornate ivory handle. That again sets it apart – the tang of an earlier dagger would almost certainly have been carved from wood or bone."

"Excellent!" exclaimed Holmes, "And to what purpose would such a dagger have been used?"

"The nature of the long and tapered blade made this weapon ideal for thrusting and puncturing, much like the later stiletto knife. By the fifteenth century, it had become the favoured side-arm of medieval knights, who would use it in hand to hand combat. A rondel dagger could be forced between the joints of a suit of armour or used with deadly effect to penetrate chain mail. However, most of the highly-decorated rondels which we see preserved in collections today would have been commissioned purely for ceremonial purposes. Beyond the medieval battlefield, the rondel emerged as a fashionable item, displayed at the waist of wealthy middle class merchants and artisans across Europe. The inlaid decoration on this ivory handle hint at that earlier ritualistic function, and I can say with some confidence that this dagger has been produced as one of a limited batch for a small and secretive band of men."

I could see that my conclusion had piqued Holmes's interest. "Indeed, Mr Mickleburgh. And would I be right in suggesting that this select society is known as the *Bosworth Order*?"

"You would, although I know little about the organisation beyond its adoption of this type of dagger. I have seen only one before, which belonged to the father of a student I briefly shared a room with at Cambridge. Lester Devlin invited me to his palatial home in Huntingdon one weekend and - knowing my keen interest in medieval weaponry - made a great fuss of showing me, rather covertly, into his father's study. Housed within a secure glass cabinet was a display of three rondel daggers, one identical to this. While the other two weapons looked to be genuine fourteenth century pieces, the smaller rondel was clearly a much later reproduction. As I said as much, Devlin's father entered the study and with some annoyance announced that I was absolutely correct. Before being shepherded away, Hugh Devlin casually let it slip that there were only eight such daggers in existence and each belonged to members of the Bosworth Order. When I later quizzed Lester about the connection, he knew little beyond the fact that the order was a secret society to which his father had been a member. The dagger was apparently given to those initiated into the order. Beyond that, I can tell you no more, Mr Holmes."

"My dear fellow, your academic reputation is clearly deserved and the additional information you have provided about the connection to the Devlin family is invaluable."

"Then, could I ask, Mr Holmes, how you already knew that the dagger was used by the Bosworth Order?"

Holmes powerful gaze dropped momentarily towards the floor. When he raised his head, a look of some concern had crept across his pallid features. "I see no reason why I should not take you into my trust, Mr Mickleburgh, but you must agree to treat the matters I relay as highly confidential. Can I depend upon your discretion?"

I gave him every assurance that I could be trusted and sat back to listen to his disclosure. It was a most remarkable tale.

"Yesterday lunchtime, I received a telegram from my brother Mycroft, who works for the British Government. He asked me to attend a hastily convened meeting at the Foreign and Commonwealth Office in Whitehall. When I arrived, I was told that a foreign diplomat had been murdered at his home in Stoke Newington the previous night, the body found the following morning by the dead man's butler. Due to the nature of the crime, the ministers and civil servants present had determined that a private and discreet inquiry would be preferable to a general investigation by Scotland Yard. On Mycroft's recommendation, I was asked to carry out that inquiry. I requested only that the scene of the crime be left as the butler had found it.

"Within two hours, I had travelled by train from Liverpool Street station to Stoke Newington and found myself within a two-wheeled trap approaching the small Tudor mansion of the late Edward Flanders, agent-general of the crown colony of New South Wales in Australia. In the fading light of the afternoon, I first explored the grounds around the house and then examined each of the downstairs rooms of the property, before asking Mr Peters, the butler, to show me the corpse. The body lay, where it had been found, on the carpet of the ground floor bed chamber where Flanders normally slept. He lay on his back, his feet pointing towards the French windows, which provided access to the garden of the estate and a point of entry for the killer. The rondel dagger had been thrust into his chest and he had fallen back to die where he lay. He was dressed in flannel pyjamas, a long red dressing gown and black carpet slippers. On the floor to his right was an iron poker. I spent twenty minutes examining the body and searching the room and then explained to the butler that Whitehall had made arrangements for a coroner to be notified and the body to be taken away later that day."

I could not help but interject. "Do you believe the poker was first used to stun the man, before the dagger was deployed?"

"No," replied Holmes. "It was Flanders who had been carrying the poker, no doubt armed for the encounter with our assailant. He had been expecting the intrusion you see."

"I'm not sure I do, Mr Holmes. Are you saying that he was disturbed during the night, arose from his bed and went over to challenge whoever it was trying to enter the house through the French windows?"

"Not quite. There is no fireplace in the downstairs bed chamber. It was clear to me that Flanders had been sleeping in an upstairs room at the time. On hearing a noise downstairs, he had put on the dressing gown and slippers and armed himself with the poker. Mr Peters later confirmed that Flanders had been sleeping upstairs for the previous three nights, but had given no explanation for his sudden reluctance to use the downstairs bed chamber."

"But if he was expecting an intruder, why did he not confide in Peters and ask him to be more vigilant in checking the security of the ground floor?"

"A key question and an excellent line of enquiry – why indeed? Well, I found the answer within an unlocked desk drawer. Flanders's study adjoins the downstairs bed chamber and having searched the main bureau within it, I found a short, handwritten note, apparently sent a week earlier. It read simply: '*Your membership has been revoked. Expect a visit. Ensure you are alone. Important matters to be discussed.*' A rubber stamp had been used to complete the communiqué. Beneath a crest bearing the arms of King Richard III, were the words '*Bosworth Order*'."

"Why do you think the killer waited a few nights before seeking out Flanders?" I then asked.

"Fear of observation, I suspect. If, like me, the killer had to travel from town on the Stoke Newington and Edmonton line, he would have been keen to make the journey without attracting unwanted attention. The weather conditions provided the perfect cover. You may remember, two nights ago, that the coal fog we have endured for some weeks now was particularly dense and extended well beyond the central London area, drifting north of the Thames in huge waves of choking smog. It provided a perfect cloak of anonymity."

"And did you discover any further clues to the identity of the killer, Mr Holmes?"

"Only that he wore gloves and carried a heavy bludgeon in addition to the dagger. He is a strong and agile right-handed man, whose height is around five feet, seven inches, and he speaks with a west highland accent. I also believe he may be partially deaf."

"So, you have detained the suspect already?"

"No. But I have every confidence that I shall do so, very soon."

I looked at him, confused. "Then I do not understand how you can know so much about the man."

His response was delivered with no hint of conceit: "Facts, Mr Mickleburgh - easily discernible facts. There were no prints or marks on the grip of the dagger, suggesting gloves. The weapon had been driven upwards and into the left side of Flanders's sternum with considerable force and some speed. So much so, that - although armed with an iron poker and anticipating possible violence - the victim had been unable to deflect or respond to the lunge of the dagger. This also tells us that the attacker came to kill rather than talk, despite the wording of the note. Flanders was a tall man, well over six feet in height. The weapon's point of entry suggested an assailant somewhat shorter and right-handed.

"The killer had gained entry to the locked chamber with no great skill or finesse, smashing a small pane of the French windows in a single blow, to then reach inside and unlock the doors. I suspect this was the sound which first roused Flanders. The punched hole in the glass bore the distinct hallmarks of the round end of a heavy wooden bludgeon. As for his accent, the clue came from the rose bushes which adorn the south-facing wall of the manor house, close to the French windows. Our man had strayed a little too close to the prickly branches, leaving tell-tale strands of cloth clinging to the thorns. I have made it my business to recognise all the main variants of tweed and tartan cloth, and recognised the weft and weave in this case to be the distinct green and black sett of the 'Black Watch' tartan, worn by the Clan Campbell and other west highland families. While it is possible that the fellow was dressed in tartan trousers, I think it more likely that he wore a kilt, which would more easily explain the snagging on the roses."

I stood in awe of the man's uncanny abilities, but could not resist a final enquiry. "And the assertion that he's partially deaf?"

"Oh yes, a detail I overlooked. More of a punt; but when I approached the manor house yesterday afternoon, I could hear a distinct barking from three or four dogs kennelled at the back of the house. Peters explained later that these are the gun dogs which Flanders kept for his weekend shooting parties. It was clear that the beasts had been alerted by the approach of the trap along the gravel path, and they continued to bark as I walked around the outside of the house searching for clues. I am sure that they would have responded equally as noisily hearing our intruder skulking around the estate. Most would-be assassins might have been put off by any such commotion, but our man appeared to carry on regardless."

I have met many intelligent, articulate and distinguished characters in my academic career, but can say with all honesty that Sherlock Holmes eclipsed them all. And I realised in that moment that I wanted to work alongside him in the future, offering whatever assistance I could in tackling the cases and conundrums he faced. My challenge was how best to broach the matter. In the event, I opted for a short-term proposal: "Mr Holmes, I appreciate your candour in sharing with me the details of this case and your findings to date. It strikes me that I could still prove useful to you in getting to the heart of this affair. I am due some leave from my researches and could easily arrange to take some time away from the museum, if you would permit me to be an unpaid, yet willing, assistant."

Holmes raised himself from the armchair and stood for a few seconds looking deeply into the flames of the fire. His eyes were deep-set and for the first time I noticed the dark rings above his cheek line. When he finally glanced over and addressed me, a distinct grin lit up his otherwise expressionless face. "That is a very kind offer which, ordinarily, I would have declined. In this case, I do believe that you could prove useful with my continuing inquiry. If your leave can be arranged in the next ten minutes, you could indeed accompany me to my next port of call."

"And where might that be?" I enquired.

"Whitehall – my brother Mycroft is expecting to hear how the case is progressing.

\*\*\*\*\*\*\*\*\*\*\*\*\*\*\*\*\*\*\*\*\*\*\*\*

It was a simple matter to arrange to take three days away from the museum. I wrote a short note to Dr Spencer, the curator in charge of my department, and placed it in an envelope on his desk. The elderly gentleman was rarely at the museum in any case, as he suffered periodically from bouts of both gout and rheumatism. I was certain that my short absence would not concern him.

When Holmes and I emerged from the museum, we found that there had been no further deposits of snow and the skies had cleared sufficiently to allow for a hint of warmth from the winter sun. The streets around us were bathed in light and the pavements were bustling with all manner of visitors, tradesmen and loiterers. With the lingering nip in the air, I turned up the collar on my frock coat and followed Holmes as he set off down Great Russell Street. Discounting the use of a cab, he suggested that we walk the mile and a half from Bloomsbury, through High Holborn, and along the Charing Cross Road to Whitehall.

It was close to nine-thirty as we approached the grand white façade of the government building that Mycroft Holmes occupied. On our walk, his brother had been reticent to share any further details about the man beyond saying that Mycroft was "...a key player within the mechanism of government" and "...a conduit for vital information and intelligence across all of the Whitehall departments". I got the distinct impression that while there was a grudging respect on both sides, theirs was peculiarly brotherly relationship with evident sibling rivalry.

I found Mycroft to be both welcoming and urbane in his plush civil service office, bedecked with oak panelling and luxurious leather armchairs. He seemed enthusiastic when told that I was assisting his brother. While a little more thickset than Sherlock and some three or four inches shorter in height, there was no mistaking the familial look. His conversation was direct, witty and effortless and after exchanging a few pleasantries and inviting us to join him for a small glass of sherry, he asked what progress had been made on the case.

Sherlock expounded on the key features and the facts he had ascertained from his visit to Stoke Newington and then gave an outline description of the suspect. He also explained how he had brought me into the inquiry, the significance of the rondel dagger and the likely links to the Bosworth Order. Mycroft listened intently – his eyes closed for much of the time - keen to catch every word and nuance and interjecting at times in order to ensure that he fully understood all of the information given.

When all of the pertinent facts had been presented, Mycroft looked very directly at his brother, smiled benignly and then asked with sincerity: "What now, Sherlock? How does the investigation proceed from here?"

The detective's reply took me by surprise. "Well, Mycroft. You might like to start being a little more open with me about why there is so much sensitivity surrounding this death. Was the diplomat leading some sort of double life? Were you already aware of his links to the Bosworth Order? Had you already anticipated an attempt on his life? There is clearly some backdrop to this case which you have chosen not to share with me."

In spite of the pithy and brusque nature of the challenge, Mycroft responded with admirable composure. "As ever, dear brother, you are prone to trample headlong into the mire of government affairs and diplomatic sensitivities. I can see that you are not likely to be persuaded by any artifice on my part, so I will be straight with you. Mr Mickleburgh, I would ask that you must also treat what you are about to hear as confidential."

I nodded in consent and, with a final sip of his sherry, Mycroft then began to explain.

"It may come as some surprise to you to learn that this country's relationship with our colonial cousins in Australia has not always been as close as we would have liked. The continent has been strategically important for Britain, offering, as it does, vast amounts of new land for farming and access to an untapped wealth of mineral deposits and other raw materials that our empire has hungrily consumed. And yet, our only real solution to the problem of how best to provide the essential labour to unlock the potential of these lands was, until a decade or so ago, to send the crown colonies a constant source of convict labour – an approach which has done little to endear us to the diligent settlers and British investors who have sunk many hundreds of thousands of pounds of their hard-earned capital down under.

"Many of the crown colonies are now acutely aware that their interests and those of the mother country do not entirely match and, while there are distinct differences in attitude across the continent, Her Majesty's Government has become concerned about the growth in nationalism and open talk of separatism in some quarters. At the same time, ministers are not immune to the need for the colonies to expand their economic and trading activities across the globe. Edward Flanders had been most helpful in this respect. In his diplomatic role, dividing his time equally between his Australian home and his retreat in Stoke Newington, he had worked ceaselessly to put New South Wales at the forefront of a new rapprochement with Britain; developing new trading links, stimulating fresh investment and encouraging migrant workers from across the empire to settle in the territory. In particular, he has been instrumental in creating an export market in Britain for Australian beef and lamb.

"With our expanding population and the problems with domestic farming – in particular, the consistently poor harvests in recent years and the reductions in our livestock herds from persistent cattle plagues – we have welcomed these new food imports. At first, the Australians pioneered the export of canned meat, but after a few unsuccessful attempts, they succeeded last year in transporting the first 40 tons of frozen beef and mutton from Sydney on board the *Strathleven*. Backed by the efforts of Flanders, these shipments are expected to grow exponentially.

"As you might imagine, there has not been a universally positive response to this development and, alongside some hostility from the other crown colonies, Edward Flanders has come under attack from a number of pro-British establishment figures and some prominent agriculturalists. While we were aware that he has faced some vitriolic verbal assaults in Parliament and in the press, we had not imagined that his life might be in danger. For that reason, I thought it best that his untimely death was investigated most sensitively in the first instance - hence your involvement."

"Thank you, Mycroft, that is understood, although I do not see why you could not have shared this with me much earlier," said Sherlock, his response seeming almost petulant.

With that, he rose from his seat, placed his sherry glass in the middle of Mycroft's desk and made for the door.

Mycroft cast me a glance, winked and then shouted after his brother, "I'll wait to hear of any further developments then…"

***********************

Outside in the busy pell-mell that is Whitehall, Holmes said nothing further about the meeting with Mycroft. Instead, he set off once more at a brisk pace, his cane swinging out before him like an inverted metronome. My casual enquiry about our intended destination brought only two clipped words: "Covent Garden".

Twenty minutes later, I found myself, once more, in a lavishly furnished room, this time the lounge bar of the Garrick Club. Holmes announced that he was looking for an acquaintance within the club and sauntered off in pursuit of the man. I busied myself with a couple of newspapers and ordered a coffee.

When he returned to the lounge, his mood appeared to be greatly improved.

"A useful discussion?" I ventured.

"Yes, indeed," came the reply. "I sought out a former client, Sir James Fitzjames Stephen, the High Court judge. He is not only a most competent lawyer, but something of a specialist on secret societies and ancient orders. I asked him if he knew of the Bosworth Order and he laughed."

"Really?!"

"Yes, it seems clear to me now why I have never heard of the organisation. James explained that the Bosworth Order was a short-lived gentlemen's drinking club which gained some notoriety in the 1850s as a house of ill-repute. It operated for only two years and catered almost exclusively for the sons of a small number of wealthy industrialists who excelled at drinking, gambling and fraternising with ladies of easy virtue. There was always a limit to the numbers of members who could join the club, each new entrant being required to complete a secret initiation ritual, which included the receipt of a ceremonial rondel dagger. To his knowledge, there were never more than a handful of members of the club."

"So, we were wrong to assume that it was an ancient order?"

"Yes, and certainly less high-brow than I had anticipated. I think our next step must be to speak to the father of your student friend, Lester Devlin, and see if he can shed any further light on the members of this notorious drinking den. Are you happy to accompany me to Huntingdon? I assume that the family still lives there?"

I was delighted at the prospect and thrilled that I could still be of use. I confirmed that the family did indeed continue to live on the outskirts of Huntingdon – Lester had recently written to me while visiting his parents. Ordinarily he was stationed abroad, working on the Continent as the estate manager for a major French vineyard.

Our rail journey from King's Cross to Huntingdon on the Great Northern line took us about two hours and we chatted constantly whilst enjoying a most excellent meal in the train's new and much publicised dining car. Saying little more about the case, Holmes seemed content to explicate his distinctive approach to problem solving.

"I always begin with *research*, Mr Mickleburgh. As our Prime Minister, Mr Disraeli, said, some years ago: 'It is knowledge that influences and equalises the social condition of man...' I keep extensive files and card indexes on all manner of crimes and criminals, but my starting point on any case is to carry out whatever legwork and early research I can, from whatever sources are available to me. In this way, I had already discovered, before we even met, that you are thirty-seven years of age and the youngest of six siblings born to a well-regarded farming family in Thrandeston, Suffolk. After attending the Mistley School in Manningtree, you read Classics at Cambridge University and since graduation have worked in various academic capacities. You have lived alone in your rented Montague Street house since joining the British Museum, although a nearby neighbour has observed that you recently took in two stray cats."

"I had no idea that my rather limited existence could be so easily exposed."

"We do not exist without leaving tangible footprints, traces, remnants and records of our fleeting, yet closely interwoven, lives, my dear fellow. Remember John Donne's devotional phrase: 'No man is an island'. Every breath, step, touch and conversation we experience has the potential to leave its mark, if only in the memory of another. Solid research can help to expose some of that, but I have also trained myself to spot the almost imperceptible clues that others may overlook. Hence, the second essential phase of my approach, *observation*."

"And what have you observed of me, Mr Holmes."

"The obvious; you are roughly six feet, two inches tall with fair hair, hazel-coloured eyes and a distinctly sallow complexion. You are left-handed, walk with a slight limp in your right leg and can be generally ungainly in most your movements."

I laughed at the last of his observations. "No doubt, you have spoken to one of my family in gathering that vital piece of information? It is frequently spoken of by them, that I am something of a lumbering oaf."

Holmes looked at me askance. "No, Mr Micklebugh. It is purely an observation, although had I enjoyed any such communication with your family, it would have been a useful confirmation of what I had observed. You see, observation without solid facts can sometimes lead us into the hazardous world of assumptions, speculation and guesswork. As such, the next phase of my approach is to weigh-up what I have learned from research with what is discernible through observation. In that way, I am able to draw empirical *links* between the data."

"Rather like forming a working hypothesis," I ventured.

"Exactly that, my friend - and it is the sensible working hypothesis which can lead to the *evaluation* or conclusion of our studies. Let me illustrate this in your case. I can see that you have two distinct, parallel abrasions on your left hand. The cuts are only skin deep. I had learnt earlier that you now have two cats, both of which had previously survived on the street. It is not such a leap of faith to conclude that the cuts are claw marks from one of the animals which has yet to adapt itself to its newfound home and guardian."

"Bravo! That is accurate in every respect. What else?"

"Well, a look at your expensive ankle boots reveals that you are clearly not meticulous in polishing the leather. With respect, they do not look well cared for at all. My knowledge of your status and profession tells me that it is not your day to day work or lack of resources which has led to this situation. Combined with the information that you grew up in an agricultural family as the youngest of six children, it is easy to conclude that there was always an older brother at hand to polish your footwear as you grew up, and this has created in you a degree of slothfulness in such matters which has stayed with you into adulthood."

I took no offence at his remarks and could only smile at his pinpoint accuracy. "I find this both intriguing and enlightening. Is there anything further?"

"Yes, if you wish. The yellow stains on your left index finger, tell me that you are a smoker and, primarily, a cigarette smoker. The slight staining on your teeth reveals, furthermore, that you have smoked for some years. The discarded ash I observed in the ashtray of your room confirmed that Wild Woodbines are your preferred cigarettes."

"Oh, that was too simple! With knowledge of your methods, I think even I might have worked that out."

Holmes looked to be enjoying this and was clearly up for the challenge. "In that case, I will reveal that I know you to have been a keen and award-winning rugby football player."

"Now, *that* I do find remarkable. If I am again to believe that you have not spoken to my family, I know not how you could have discerned the information. I have never spoken of my passion for the sport at work and have not touched a ball since leaving university."

"Again, a simple matter of linking a few basic facts and observations; the obvious limp and the very visible evidence that you have at some stage suffered a broken nose, and have what doctors might refer to as a complication of the *perichondrial hematoma*, more commonly known as a 'cauliflower ear'. The damage to this external portion of the ear is most frequently to be seen on prize fighters. I know this because I am something of an accomplished pugilist myself. And yet, your knuckles do not bear the perceptible scars of a boxer. I am aware that Mistley School was one of the earliest adopters of the Rugby School style of football and conclude, therefore, that it was at rugby that you sustained all of these injuries – ailments which may also, of course, account for your somewhat cumbersome gait."

"Astonishing, simply astonishing! And, of course, you would not have failed to notice the small, unmarked, silver trophy which sits on my desk – tangible evidence of my earlier sporting prowess as 'star player' in the school rugby team during my final year. In fact, the only award I ever received at school, hence its elevated status in my limited display."

"Yes, indeed. But you are wrong to suggest that it is unmarked. In fact, the edge of the base displays the name of the maker 'R. & S. Garrard & Co.' alongside a small representation of a rugby ball."

"I confess, I have never noticed that, which again adds testimony to your exceptional observational skills. I stand in awe of your approach, Mr Holmes."

Shortly afterwards, we reached Huntingdon, set within the snow covered fields and hedgerows of its rural landscape. We climbed down from our warm carriage to face a considerable barrage of sleet and a choking haze of engine smoke, and I shivered at the unexpected drop in temperature. Luckily, it was only a short walk to the station concourse where we were able to find a convenient carriage to transport us the final two miles to Braxton Hall.

The Devlin home looked every bit as grand and ostentatious as it did when I first visited in 1863. The Jacobean manor was built on the ruins of an earlier priory and had been added to and remodelled by every subsequent generation of owners. Lester's father, Hugh Devlin, had bought the estate in 1860, having been an early investor in a long list of railway-related property developments across Britain. He had further modified Braxton Hall and its grounds into a popular and successful hunting estate. As we approached the hall along the mile-long drive, I wondered if Devlin already knew of the death of Edward Flanders.

************************

Hugh Devlin looked to have aged well beyond his fifty-five years. His hair had thinned substantially, his waistline had expanded and his eyes looked dull and bloodshot. He was gracious in receiving us, examining Holmes's calling card with keen interest, and indicating that he had never heard of a 'consulting detective'. He seemed elated to learn that I had pursued a career as an academic, readily admitting that his own son's choice of profession had more to do with Lester's fondness for the Bordeaux grape than it did for any potential to earn money. We were shown into his spacious study on the ground floor and invited to take a seat on a long davenport sofa which faced a large writing desk.

Holmes seemed impatient to get to work and declined Devlin's offer of a cognac and a Cuban cigar. At our host's direction he announced the reason for our visit. "Mr Devlin, it is kind of you to receive us at such short notice. I should explain that I am investigating the murder of a former colleague of yours, Mr Edward Flanders."

There was no ambiguity in Devlin's reaction. It was quite clear that this was news to him and he appeared to be momentarily thunderstruck. Holmes waited a short while before continuing: "I am sorry to be so direct, but you will understand the pressing need to get to the bottom of this heinous crime. Mr Flanders was slain at his residence in

Stoke Newington and had received a warning of sorts prior to the attack. I would therefore be extremely grateful if you could tell me more about the unexpected note that you received this morning from the Bosworth Order."

A look of unchecked anger flashed across Devlin's face. "How dare you, sir! I received you in good faith, as you arrived in the company of Mr Mickleburgh, the only student friend of Lester's that I ever had any respect for. And yet, you betray that faith by asking me of a matter that you can only have known about either by spying on me, or by intercepting my correspondence. I have a full armoury of shotguns and will have no hesitation in..."

"Hugh! Please!" I felt it my duty to intercede on Holmes's behalf. "My colleague is an honourable and trustworthy fellow, of that I can assure you. His investigatory abilities are quite remarkable and he possesses many singular talents which set him apart from any academic or professional man I have ever met. If you would hear the man out, I am certain that he will explain how he knows of the note. Flanders had also received a note in recent days, you see."

Devlin looked unconvinced and turned sharply towards Holmes once more. "Very well, sir! I am all ears!"

"There is no particular mystery or deceit to this. My role requires me to piece together the knowable, observable and logical facts of any case in order to draw conclusions. Mr Mickleburgh is correct in what he says. A few days ago, Edward Flanders received an unexpected note from someone purporting to represent the Bosworth Order, the short-lived gentlemen's club that the two of you were members of some years ago. In Flanders's case, the note preceded his demise, and I believe that the author and the assailant are one in the same man. Flanders had been stabbed with a rondel dagger as if to emphasise the importance of the connection to the club. It seemed logical to me that you may have known something of the matter or, indeed, have been confronted with a similar threat from this attacker."

I could see that all of this had struck a chord with Devlin, whose expression was once again one of perplexity. "Yes...eh...yes, Mr Holmes. I see. I was too quick to judge. But how did you know that I received the note today?"

"We sit in your study. In the bay window is your writing desk which I walked past and scrutinised as you invited me to take a seat. It is clear that you sit at your desk in dealing with all of your regular correspondence. The accoutrements of this endeavour are plain to see; the envelopes, foolscap, ink pen and paper knife. This is a grand house in which your domestic staff would take it upon themselves to empty the waste paper basket you have beside the desk on a daily basis. So, to see the torn remnants of a familiar cream envelope and what remains of its distinctive wax seal, can only mean that you received a note - very much like that received by Flanders - earlier today."

"I am dumbfounded by what you say, sir. And you must forgive my somewhat rash response earlier, but I have been on my guard since receiving the note. It is clear that you already know something of the Bosworth Order, but I imagine that the precise nature of the threat involved may not be quite so obvious?"

Holmes was forthright in his reply. "Quite so – although I am certain that our assailant has an Australian connection. How else would he have known about Flanders's return to Britain, when a number of Whitehall departments had sought to keep his fleeting visit to Stoke Newington a closed guarded secret?"

"Well, there is some backdrop to this tale, Mr Holmes, and the Australian continent does indeed feature prominently within it. But let me start from the beginning." He arose from his desk and took a small key from his waistcoat, before approaching a large bureau to our left. "I have not opened this cabinet for a while. At one time, it was my pride and joy. A cherished collection of medieval daggers – added to in number since Mr Mickleburgh was here last – in the centre of which sits my favourite; the first rondel dagger I had, given to me as part of the initiation for the Bosworth Order. A foolish, youthful indiscretion, but a history I cannot now deny."

Having opened two heavy oak doors on the bureau, the glass cabinet housing the collection of daggers was revealed. I looked at the collection in awe, recognising at once the rarity and exquisite craftsmanship of the dozen or so weapons he had collected, which were positioned around the ivory-handled imposter.

"It was my idea to have a ceremonial dagger, to signify one's allegiance to the club. It also served as a tangible reminder to anyone thinking of betraying the trust we shared. A trust that was essential in maintaining the secrecy of what we indulged in behind closed doors. Drunken debauchery, gambling and sin of every kind – the very worst excesses, like some bacchanalian orgy. Had the club not been forced to close, in order to avert an investigation by Scotland Yard, it is likely that we would all have died in one way or another. When the club closed its doors, we all went our separate ways; most of us settling to the humdrum existence of family life in the shires. For a few, however, the break would prove to be ruinous.

"The club was originally inspired by Edward Flanders and two of his chums from Eton, who had earlier formed a clandestine society with pretentions towards the Knights

Templar. They began to cultivate a wider group of young men, who would come together to discuss lofty topics of a historical nature over a few glasses of fine port. By the time I joined them in the early summer of 1852, the academic posturing had all but gone, with the main order of ceremonies revolving around a heady mixture of gaming and drinking.

"That same summer, we were joined by a newcomer who was to assert himself within the group and, ultimately, claim a role as general secretary of the club, or 'Clan Chief' as he liked to refer to himself. By this time, there were eight of us, almost all of whom were the sons of self-made men; industrialists, merchants, professional types, in fact, anyone other than the landed gentry. But even here, our Clan Chief stood apart. James Campbell-Grant was descended from a long line of canny Scots who still held sway in the west highlands and he stood to inherit a fortune with the passing of his elderly father."

Holmes turned to me briefly, raising his eyebrows, and then responded. "That is fascinating to hear, Mr Devlin. And did Mr Campbell-Grant ever have occasion to wear a kilt?"

"Never out of one, Mr Holmes. In fact, I cannot recollect ever seeing him in a pair of trousers. He was passionate about his homeland and fiercely loyal to his Argyll family. It was he who named our group the 'Bosworth Order' and negotiated the lease on the Pall Mall premises in which we met. He expected all of us to be dedicated to the club in the same way that he was to his ancestral roots."

"Is it not strange," queried Holmes, "that a passionate Scot should be minded to create a drinking club in honour of such a prominent English king?"

Hugh Devlin laughed. "I think his choice of name was ironic. Campbell-Grant was no lover of English kings from what I can remember."

At this point I interposed. "I think there may be more to the name than you imagine. While many prominent west highland families gave support to the Crown throughout the fifteenth century, few would have rallied to Richard's cause at the Battle of Bosworth because of his bloody incursions into Scotland from 1480. Henry Tudor, on the other hand, bolstered the ranks of his rebel army with professional soldiers from Scotland, Wales and France. There is a strong element of folklore which suggests that before he received his fatal wounds on the battlefield of Bosworth in 1485, Richard had been stabbed in the head by a rondel dagger wielded by a Scottish mercenary."

Devlin's face lit up at this point. "Now you say that, I do remember that Campbell-Grant was particularly smitten with my idea of a ceremonial weapon and insisted that the design should be that of a rondel dagger. He may well have subscribed to the same theory."

"Excellent!" exclaimed Holmes. "Your academic expertise has proved invaluable once more, Mr Mickleburgh! But let us continue, Mr Devlin..."

"Indeed. In October 1854, our numbers had fallen to six. One club member had died of cholera that summer and another had succumbed to the effects of alcohol poisoning, passing away a few days before his twenty-second birthday. And then Campbell-Grant received word of the impending police investigation. He would never reveal who had first alerted him to the threat, but within a week the word went out and our meetings stopped. I believed that the Bosworth Order would cease to operate from that point on."

"And yet it did not, Mr Devlin. You all went your separate ways, but I perceive that some of the ties you had were not so easy to disentangle? You see, I find it fascinating that all the way through your account you have referred to Campbell-Grant in the *past tense*. As if the fellow had vanished from the face of the earth. But we know that not to be the case. This story hinges on an event or series of events that occurred in the aftermath of the club's demise and which resulted in Campbell-Grant's criminal conviction and transportation to Australia. That is so, is it not, Mr Devlin?"

He could not hide his astonishment and stubbed out what remained of his cigar. "You have an uncanny ability, Mr Holmes, I will grant you that. How could you know? Only Flanders and I knew the truth of what went on in 1855. We pledged to take our secret to the grave; something I imagine poor Edward has done..."

Holmes looked at him solemnly. "I do not yet know the detail of what occurred between you all, but you admitted to the Australian connection earlier. There is only one place that a man could travel to on that continent which might immediately render him as dead or forgotten in the minds of those who previously knew him. That place has to be the penal colony – the destination for so many criminals convicted in this country."

"There is no denying it, sir. The past has indeed come back to haunt me. When the club disbanded, both Flanders and I saw it as something of a blessing. Unlike the other members, the pair of us had both lost heavily at the card table and had accumulated debts which we stood little chance of paying off. All of the money was owed to Campbell-Grant, who had bankrolled our debts, no doubt seeking to exert his influence over us for some years to come. Naïvely, we believed that he would write off the sums owed with the collapse of the club.

33

But within a matter of weeks, both of us received letters from the man indicating that he expected full repayment.

"Fearing financial ruin, we hatched a plan to outwit Campbell-Grant. Flanders fabricated a burglary at his west London townhouse and planted a few of the gold and silver items that he claimed had been stolen, in the Scotsman's Kensington apartment. I provided testimony that I had not only seen Campbell-Grant entering the townhouse, but had also seen him making off with some of the 'stolen' pieces. The case went to trial at the Old Bailey and Campbell-Grant found himself facing the formidable prosecuting barrister, Sir Hilary Grantham. He was found guilty and sentenced to transportation. Afterwards, he spent about a year in Millbank Prison and was then transported to Van Diemen's Land to serve a term of fourteen years hard labour in the colony."

"And you thought that would be the last you would hear of him?" said Holmes. There was a hint of condescension in his voice.

"Yes, as far as Flanders and I were concerned, he was gone forever. We both got on with our lives and went our separate ways. Flanders initially pursued a career in the civil service and later prospered in Australia. I have occasionally read of his exploits in the press. I married, bought this estate and raised a family. Campbell-Grant lost his liberty and his fortune – when his conviction was confirmed, his family disowned him and his father took steps to ensure that he would never inherit their Scottish estates. I take no pride in admitting that I ruined the man's life, so entertain few doubts that he now wishes to see me dead. When I received the note this morning, I realised that it could only have been sent by the Clan Chief."

Prompted by Holmes, Devlin went on to reveal the substance of the note; word for word, the same message as that received by Flanders.

Holmes moved on to practical matters. "We have clearly managed to pre-empt any attack that Campbell-Grant may be planning, but I would not underestimate the lengths that this wronged man may go to in exacting his revenge. The light outside is fading fast and will provide him with sufficient cover should he plan to strike tonight. Mr Devlin, I would ask that you carry on as you would, had none of this come to light, and to instruct your domestic staff to do the same, albeit that I would like them to lock every door and secure all of the downstairs windows. It would also be helpful if you could leave the doors of your display cabinet open, with the medieval daggers on display. For our part, Mr Mickleburgh and I will keep out of sight and attempt to foil any such intrusion."

For the next hour, Holmes led me on a swift but thorough reconnaissance of the ground floor of the hall, noting each point of entry, testing every lock and window catch and scouting out possible weaknesses in the seemingly secure property. As the curtains to most rooms were pulled across and lamps lit throughout the house, he was careful to ensure that we could not be observed from the grounds of Braxton Hall. I was thrilled to be alongside him, enjoying every minute of the unfolding adventure and secretly lamenting the fact that I would, at some point soon, need to return to my dreary academic life.

Around eight o'clock that evening we were invited to join Hugh Devlin for a hearty meal of venison and roasted potatoes. He explained that rooms had been prepared for us to sleep at the hall that night. I took a large glass of Burgundy with the meal and afterwards began to regret it, feeling suddenly weary from all of the day's exertions. Holmes, I noted, seemed content to pick at his food with no great enthusiasm and declined the offer of any liquid refreshment. The conversation was cordial but distinctly low key and I found myself doing most of the talking, explaining to our host the nature of my academic work. At half-past nine, Devlin announced that he was retiring for the night and left us in the dining room.

Holmes seemed to have a firm plan of action. Leaving the domestic staff to clear the dining room, he suggested we head back to Devlin's study. My apparent lethargy had also been noted: "It could be a long night, Mr Mickleburgh. You may wish to grab forty winks on the davenport. I will nudge you awake should anything occur."

It was approaching midnight when I was roused from my heavy slumber, surprised to find that the room was awash with light and more than a little chilly. I realised that Holmes had opened one of two sets of heavy curtains in the room to reveal a full moon in the clear and starry sky. I could also see that one of the two long sash windows facing me was open three or four inches. Holmes said nothing but moved his gloved hand to my lips. Dutifully, I nodded, acknowledging the request for silence, and raised myself from the sofa. Holmes then moved swiftly, but noiselessly, around to the back of the sofa. I did likewise, and then kept my body and head tucked down out of view.

It was two or three minutes later when I heard the distinct sound of the sash window being raised. Even without a view, I could tell that someone was attempting to enter the room. Presently, I heard a light footfall on the wooden floorboards and perceived that our intruder was heading across the floor in the direction of Devlin's display cabinet to our left.

I glanced forward at Holmes and realised that he sat, poised at the ready, the silver-topped cane gripped firmly in his left hand. There then followed an almighty thump and the breaking of glass. At that instant, Holmes leapt to his feet and made towards the man, who stood with his back to us, seemingly unaware that he was about to be challenged. He was shorter than Holmes, well-built and wearing an Inverness cape and tartan tam-o'-shanter. His right arm was held across the front of his chest and I could see in his gloved hand the heavy wooden cudgel that he had just used to smash the glass. Campbell-Grant at last!

Holmes raised his cane and brought the weighty silver pommel down hard on the Scotsman's wrist. In the evident surprise of the moment, Campbell-Grant dropped the cudgel and let out an almighty roar. He swung round, clutching the injured wrist to his chest, and then tried to launch himself at Holmes, his left hand flailing in a wild attempt to connect with the detective's jaw. As I moved forward, I watched Holmes deftly side-step the attempted punch, while sending his own right fist thundering into the side of Campbell-Grant's head. The stocky figure slumped to the floor.

"Bravo, Mr Holmes!" I exclaimed, standing over the body of the unconscious man and noticing for the first time the tartan kilt that he wore beneath the cape. "You are indeed an accomplished pugilist!"

"Aided by the fact that the man clearly did not hear me coming – it seems he is hard of hearing after all!" Holmes looked ecstatic and stooped to check the pulse of the floored intruder.

I could hear the sound of voices and movement elsewhere in the house, the noise of the breaking glass and scuffle having evidently raised some of the domestic staff.

"How could you be sure that he would use the open window?" I enquired. "Did you not fear that he might suspect some sort of ruse or snare?"

Holmes beamed at me. "The fellow is headstrong and irrational, and driven by the rage and injustice he feels. You accompanied me when I scouted out the place earlier – the hall is very nearly impregnable. I knew that he would not ignore the potentially easy entrance, whatever the risk. I watched him trek through the heavy snow outside, keeping close to the yew trees which line the right flank of the garden. It was only a matter of time before he found the open window. And in opening the curtains to the moonlight, I was careful to ensure that the collection of rondel daggers could be seen very clearly from the window. The opportunity to stab Devlin with the man's own ceremonial dagger was too much of a temptation – the Scot had already used his own dagger in killing Edward Flanders, you see."

At that point, the door to the study was flung open and a bleary-eyed Hugh Devlin entered carrying a hurricane lamp. Two male servants were behind him; one half-dressed in black trousers and an unbuttoned white shirt, the other still clad in his bed-clothes. Holmes immediately despatched the more suitably attired under-butler to call for a doctor and to alert the local constabulary about the break-in. His heavy-lidded assistant was tasked with making a pot of strong black coffee.

Devlin was effusive in his praise for what Holmes had done. The detective himself continued to look down at Campbell-Grant, who was now moving and showing the first signs of regaining consciousness. When Devlin had finished talking, Holmes looked up slowly and then stared at him impassively. "I rarely have any sympathy for the criminals I encounter, Mr Devlin. Understanding *why* they might have committed the acts they do, is generally only of interest to me if it aids the investigatory process and helps me to reach a point of some conclusion. And yet, in this case, I must confess to having a degree of empathy with Mr Campbell-Grant for the appalling injustice he has faced at your hands. If you have a shred of human decency within you, sir, you will make a full and honest confession to the authorities about the earlier miscarriage of justice, although I suspect it is unlikely to save this man from the gallows."

Hugh Devlin looked at him defiantly, and without a hint of self-consciousness spat back: "Go to Hell, Mr Holmes!"

The two of us remained at Braxton Hall for some hours after that and had no further contact with Devlin. We awaited the arrival of the local doctor, who tended to the very bruised and groggy James Campbell-Grant. Even when an Inspector and two burly constables from the Huntingdon County Police Force arrived an hour later to take him away, the Scotsman appeared to have little comprehension of where he was and what had transpired. Holmes and I gave short statements to Inspector Brady, who then offered to transport us to Huntingdon station in the police carriage he had arrived in. Desperately cold and in need of sleep, we boarded an early morning milk train heading for London. Some hours later, I crawled into bed back at my home in Montague Street.

It was sometime beyond lunchtime that same day when I was awoken by a sharp knocking on the front door. Tumbling out of bed, bone weary, and still wearing my clothes from the previous day, I was greeted at the door by the smiling face of Sherlock Holmes. He looked no worse for his earlier exertions and surprised me by admitting that he had yet to go to bed. "Too many loose ends to tie up, Mr Mickleburgh. I left you at the station to travel across to see Mycroft. He is, of course, delighted with the outcome of the case and reassured that

Campbell-Grant is now behind bars. It would have been embarrassing for the government had the murder been politically motivated."

"And what will happen to Devlin?" I asked, noticing that the day had warmed little since the early morning.

His face puckered. "That remains to be seen, but I doubt he will act with any spirit of contrition. Mycroft's view is that we leave him be. He is keen for a line to be drawn under the affair, so as not to attract international attention. In the meantime, I will do what I can to find out more about Campbell-Grant's detention and return from Van Diemen's Land and will acquaint you with the details in due course. I should also mention that Mycroft was very grateful for your assistance on the case."

"And you, Mr Holmes?"

He looked at me quizzically. "Yes?"

"I was just wondering how *you* felt about my involvement?"

"Well, naturally, I recognise that your academic expertise was essential in the early part of the investigation..."

Being so tired, I was always prone to say something that I might regret. And in that moment, I did exactly that and cut him short: "I'm not concerned or bothered about my *academic expertise*. What I really want to know is whether you welcomed my help as a colleague, a trusted friend, someone who could stand alongside you in times of difficulty. I have no interest in continuing to work as an academic. I had hoped that our time together might have convinced you that you needed a comrade in arms..."

Holmes looked at me, apparently lost for words. I had nothing further to add, and stood on the doorstep waiting awkwardly for him to respond. His parting words were, "Let me give it some thought." I closed the door and went back to bed, a jumbled mix of thoughts and emotions saturating my exhausted brain.

**************************

In the days that followed, I saw nothing further of Holmes. I returned to my research at the museum, to find that Dr Spencer had barely registered my absence. The snow in London had cleared, leaving just a bitterly-cold northerly wind which chilled me on my short walks into work.

It was just over a week after our return from Huntingdon that I finally received a visit from the man. Around seven o'clock that evening, I heard the distinctive rap on the door and opened it to find him clad in heavy leather boots, a long hunting jacket, thick woollen scarf and close-fitting cloth cap. Quickly, I ushered him in out of the cold and he wasted no time in getting straight to the point.

"My dear Mickleburgh. I must apologise for the time it has taken me to wrap up the Campbell-Grant case and share with you the conclusion of this sordid tale. I have, for the past week, busied myself finding out more about Campbell-Grant's transportation and passage back from Van Diemen's Land, the principal element of which was an interview with the man himself. In the event, there was not much more to tell – he had endured fourteen years hard labour and had then been released to make his own way in what was still a hostile colony. He continued to work hard, taking a job as a cattle rancher and saving whatever spare money he could in the hope that one day he could secure a passage back to England.

"After a period of over ten years, he did just that. At first he was able to travel from the colony across to mainland Australia. Having been involved in the cattle trade, he chose to settle for a few months in New South Wales and it was here that he first learned that Edward Flanders had become agent-general of the territory. Being such a high-profile figure, Flanders always seemed to be well protected and enjoyed all of the trappings that his position afforded him. Campbell-Grant determined that he would wait until Flanders made a trip back to England before attempting the murder. Within the cattle trade, it seemed to be common knowledge when Flanders planned to make these regular excursions."

"So the Scotsman really did bide his time then?" I said - keen to show I was interested in all of the new information and desperate to avoid any discussion of my behaviour when we were last together. Holmes seemed content to focus on what he had found out.

"Yes. He planned the attack on Flanders with some precision, having already gathered some relevant information on the Stoke Newington address before arriving back in England. He also revisited a family relative who had retained many of his earlier possessions, including the ceremonial rondel dagger and some of the stationery used by the Bosworth Order. Campbell-Grant told me that once he had despatched Flanders, he set out to find Devlin, taking a couple of days to discover the address in Huntingdon. He did not think for a moment that anyone would know of him or have any clue as to his mission."

"And how was the man when you spoke to him?"

"Surprisingly courteous, but resigned to his fate and not in the least bit remorseful about what he has done – an attitude which will help him little when he finally faces a judge and jury."

"I guess so. But from your point of view, I imagine this has been another successful case?"

"You may view it so, although I feel that I owe you another apology. I was not entirely straight with you earlier. Having spent some time with me, you will have learnt something of the peculiarities of my approach and the nature of my character. I do not claim to be an overtly gregarious fellow, but can be companionable with those I trust. I would ask you not to lay aside your academic career, but would be pleased to call on you to accompany me on any future cases which might benefit from your undoubted talents. You have proved yourself a most worthy associate and for that I thank you."

I found myself without words, touched to the core and forever grateful that he had called upon me that cold winter evening. I knew that it was likely to be the last time that I would stand shoulder to shoulder with the great consulting detective. What he did not realise – and what I chose not to share with him – was that I had but a short time to live. His description of my 'distinctly sallow complexion' and 'somewhat cumbersome gait' had been well observed, but misdiagnosed. In fact, it was evidence of my rapidly declining health as a result of what my doctor had diagnosed, two days earlier, as an advanced case of *Addison's disease*, an affliction of the adrenal glands.

Regaining my composure, I asked Holmes if he would like to join me for a nightcap of brandy or whisky. He declined, saying that he had an appointment with a police inspector at Scotland Yard as part of a new case concerning the mysterious disappearance of a Russian ballerina from a famous touring company. His parting words were that the case had a number of fascinating features which keenly interested him. Without further dialogue he was off, an enigmatic figure gracing the darkened streets of the Capital in pursuit of the inexplicable. I closed the door behind him and smiled - it was exactly the way that I wished to remember Mr Sherlock Holmes.

# 2. The Melancholy Methodist

When the mood took him, my good friend Sherlock Holmes possessed all the essential qualities of a showman – his face and eyes bright with enthusiasm and his hands given to such gesticulation as is necessary to draw and direct an expectant audience. His narrative was always precise and clipped, and he would pause occasionally to create tension, while varying both tone and volume to add texture and atmosphere to his delivery. In effect, he was a consummate storyteller.

It was on such an occasion that he entertained me one night with an account of an assignment he had undertaken some months before the two of us met in 1881. So singular was the tale that I have scarcely been able to forget it. And yet, I have been loath to recount the details to this point, for fear that my readers may view the narrative as overly sensational and more appropriately suited to the pages of a *penny dreadful*. That is a risk I am now prepared to take as I finally set pen to paper.

That autumn evening, we were seated comfortably before a splendid log fire in the snug lounge of a small country hotel, set within a large forested area of the Suffolk countryside. Holmes and I had just concluded a successful investigation for His Royal Highness, Prince Duleep Singh - the last Sikh Maharajah of the Punjab - who at that time owned the nearby estate of Elveden, a sizeable hunting park favoured by the nation's wealthy shooting fraternity. In his capacity as a West Suffolk magistrate, the Prince had asked Holmes to assist him with enquiries into the murder of one of the estate's gamekeepers – a straightforward enough case in which Holmes had been able to confirm the guilt of a suspect as a result of the human hairs he had taken from the barrel of the shotgun used to bludgeon the gamekeeper to death. It had later proved to be a landmark case in the developing science of forensics which my colleague had done so much to champion throughout his career.

He looked up from the fire and pointed the stem of his churchwarden towards me. There was a hint of mischievousness about his countenance as he announced suddenly that this was not the first time he had been drawn to Suffolk on a criminal case.

"You might remember my dear friend, Robert Chatton, the aged apiarist and avid book collector, who resided in Halesworth. Shortly before you and I met, Watson, he had me travel up by train to investigate the theft of a rare gem – the fifteenth century 'Ruby of Genoa', once believed to have been in the possession of the explorer, Christopher Columbus."

I had not the heart to tell him that Chatton's name rang no bells whatsoever, but nodded nevertheless.

"Chatton had inherited a small fortune with the death of a distant relative. As well as moving into Geldingbrook Hall – built originally for the Royalist sympathiser Sir Anthony Chatton - he took possession of a small but extremely valuable collection of precious stones, at the centrepiece of which was the ruby. One night that October, a small fire broke out in a stairwell of the hall. And while Chatton and his staff were quick to bring the conflagration under control, it did not take him too long to realise that the fire had been started deliberately to mask the more serious felony that had been perpetrated that evening. In short, he had been dispossessed of the Ruby of Genoa."

"I can picture the scene perfectly," I replied, taking a small sip of my brandy. "No doubt some colourful and convoluted tale unfolded thereafter..."

Holmes's face took on a look of sheer delight. "Watson, how many times do I have to remind you, not to draw conclusions when one is in possession of such scant information? In fact, this proved to be a dull and perfectly obvious affair which took me less than an hour to see through. You see there was no evidence of a break-in when I arrived the next day. It transpired that one of Chatton's maidservants had been seduced by a local tradesman, who had occasion to visit the hall on a regular basis. In doing so, he learned of the valuable gem. Thereafter, he began to visit the maid at night and had even hinted at marriage. Besotted, the young girl took him at his word and went along with his hastily conceived plan to steal the ruby on the evening in question. He convinced her to hide the gem in her attic room and to mention, if questioned, that she had seen some passing soldiers loitering around the hall earlier that week, to throw the suspicion off the domestic staff. He hoped the fire would further cover their tracks and reasoned that if the ruby was discovered, he could deny any involvement. A few interviews with the staff and a quick search of their attic quarters were all that was required to expose the truth."

"Very neat," said I. "And what happened to the pair?"

"Well, the outcome might surprise you. Chatton has always been a benevolent fellow. I believe he suspected that the robbery had been an inside job from the outset and had therefore asked for my assistance over that of the local constabulary. When the maid confessed, and the contrite tradesman was brought before us, Chatton believed that the servant was most likely to face the full force of the law for her petty treason. He told the tradesman to leave the area at once, threatening to involve the police if he ever dared to show his face again. As for the maid, he had always been impressed by her diligence and devotion to duty. She was allowed to continue in her role on the proviso that she broke off all contact with her lover and agreed never to talk of the matter again."

"Remarkable indeed. But you do not fool me, not for an instant," I exclaimed, striking a match and relighting my own pipe. "There is more to this tale than you have disclosed. It is not in your nature to recount the straightforward, obvious or run-of-the-mill. I can tell by that glint in your eye that you are working up to something else, something beyond the mundane."

My colleague stooped and began to tap out the ash from his pipe into the hearth of the fire. His face snickered as he looked up and was distracted momentarily by the sound of some other guests passing by the door of the lounge. When he fixed his attention on me, it was with the broadest of smiles. "Your intuition is commendable. I do indeed have more to share, but it is a tale of a completely different hue – a much darker matter."

"I knew it!" I could not help but interject. Holmes seemed not to mind and continued with his narrative.

"I left Geldingbrook Hall that same day. My bag was packed for a much longer visit and my very grateful friend suggested that I stay on before returning to London. I thanked Chatton, but declined his kind offer, explaining that I fancied a short trip to the coast, to revisit an old haunt. As a schoolboy, I had once spent a week crabbing and fishing in the peaceful hamlet of Walberswick and had always wished to return one day.

"Chatton arranged for a dog cart to take me to Halesworth station, where I was able to board the narrow-gauge line to Southwold. It was late in the evening as I began the short journey to the coast, across the heath and marshes of the Blyth estuary. Uncertain as to whether I would find accommodation in Walberswick itself at that hour, I took the decision to leave the train at Blythburgh and booked into the nearby *White Hart* inn, an old smugglers' den close to the magnificent fifteenth century church of the village."

I was bemused by this seemingly twee account. In the short time I had known him, I could not recollect any previous occasion on which Holmes had dwelt on any matters of a sentimental or nostalgic nature. He seemed to sense my incredulity and paused suddenly.

"Watson, the look on your face suggests that you fear I may be about to recount some long-winded travel tale. I can assure you that I am sharing these few titbits of background detail only to set the scene for what is about to come."

I took him at his word, and with a nod and a smirk settled back into my chair. He then resumed his curious monologue.

"That evening in the *White Hart* proved to be one of the most unusual I have ever experienced. With my bags deposited in an upstairs bedroom, I ventured down into the bar, eager to sample the local ale and whatever food the landlord could rustle up. A short while later, I was tucking into a sizeable steak and kidney pudding and sipping at a tall mug of winter ale.

"A few of the regulars were gathered around the fireplace of the tap room and seemed keen to entertain me with tales of local folklore. And with little to do but sit back and accept their hospitality, I was soon being regaled with stories about the legendary sea serpent of Kessingland and Blythburgh's very own devil dog, 'Black Shuck'. But it was when the conversation turned to some of the criminal exploits of the smugglers and bootleggers along the east coast that the group became most animated.

"By that stage, the weather outside the inn had deteriorated and a veritable storm had laid siege to the Blyth estuary. With the wind and rain lashing against the small panes of glass along the front of the inn, the occasional flash of lightning and deepest rumble of thunder all providing a suitably dramatic backdrop to the narratives being recounted, we were at once arrested by the opening of the main door to the inn. Pushed inside by a strong squall, a short, gaunt man stood on the threshold; his dark frame momentarily backlit by the storm. He wore a tall stove pipe hat and was dressed in a rain-soaked smock of black. In one hand he held a book, which he at once held aloft above his head, before shouting across to the six or seven of us gathered near the fire: 'He has arisen! The accursed man is back from the dead!'

"I will not embellish my narrative further, Watson, beyond saying that his entrance was not unlike something from a poorly-cast opera. Within minutes we had the bedraggled fellow seated on a wooden chair close to the hearth, his dripping-wet clothes creating a small puddle of water on the flagstones beneath his feet. With a large glass of brandy we slowly revived him from the stupor which had rapidly overcome him after his initial outburst. The bible he had been clutching now lay on a small table to his side. In an apologetic tone, the landlord whispered in my ear that the man was Evan Dyer, a Methodist minister, who lived alone in an isolated cottage at the edge of Blythburgh heath. With a liking for strong liquor and a generally gloomy outlook, he was given to regular outpourings and hysterics.

"Despite the picture painted of him, it was clear to me that Dyer had undergone a significant trauma. His eyes were wide with fear and his thin hands shook uncontrollably. The locals seemed content to let me take the lead in reviving him and making sense of what he had to say. What he eventually recounted produced that same look of fear in the eyes of all the men huddled around him. From the conversations that followed, the full story emerged.

"There had lived in the village a prize-fighter by the name of Jed Stephens. He was universally feared and loathed by the local men, being something of a ladies' man as well as a talented pugilist. While his occasional winning purses kept him in clothes, food and drink, he was forced to supplement his income with tree-cutting and hedge-laying. When sober and in regular employment, Stephens was an amiable and surprisingly devout man. He would regularly attend the Methodist chapel and for some time was taken under the wing of Evan Dyer, who believed he could reform the errant brawler. But all of that ended dramatically, when Dyer's daughter, Elizabeth – who had been staying with her estranged father on a rare familial visit – became the object of Stephen's attention and, soon after, his newfound lover. Betrayed on both fronts, Dyer took it upon himself to curse the pair - privately and in public - making clear to anyone who would listen that he believed them to be in league with the Devil."

I snorted unexpectedly, prompting Holmes to pause briefly, and eliciting from him an uneasy stare. "This has all the hallmarks of a popular melodrama, Holmes! Please tell me that you did not take any of this seriously."

He resumed his storytelling, ignoring my comments. "There were many in the village willing to believe Dyer. And as for his curses, it seemed to some that the melancholy

Methodist had genuinely raised some supernatural spirits of his own. A day after he had publicly denounced Stephens and Elizabeth as accursed servants of Beelzebub, his daughter took to her bed and died less than a week later. Stephens too succumbed to an affliction within days – a painful swelling in his upper thigh – which threatened to end his days.

"You will, no doubt, point out, Watson, that both situations are likely to have had solid medical explanations. And, of course, you would be right. The local surgeon, James Buckingham, attended both patients. He diagnosed that Elizabeth had contracted a fatal dose of English cholera and Stephens was suffering from an inflammation of the blood vessels surrounding the groin. In the latter case, it was only with some immediate and proficient arterial surgery that Dr Buckingham was able to save the pugilist's life.

"Dyer, meanwhile, continued to rant and curse Stephens, and refused to attend the burial of his daughter. She was laid to rest in the graveyard of the Blythburgh chapel in a ceremony led by the Methodist minister from Halesworth. A month later, Stephens was to join her. While the surgery had been successful, a secondary infection had apparently carried him off, much to the chagrin of the doctor.

"And how did Dyer react to the news?" I asked, now enthralled by the story.

"He maintained that both deaths were predictable, preaching that those who supped with the Devil could expect to suffer the ultimate fate. And for the two weeks following Stephens's demise, the numbers attending the chapel had swelled to capacity. It seemed that Dyer had hit a raw nerve."

"Indeed. But now I suspect you are to present me with the main part of this ghostly tale. I'm taking it from the minister's histrionics and reference to the 'accursed man' being 'back from the dead' that there is likely to be some doubt as to whether Stephens had really died?"

My friend beamed and reached for his whisky, swirling the golden liquid around in the short glass in the warm glow of the fire. "Neatly anticipated! You see, my arrival at the *White Hart* came just two weeks after the boxer's burial. That evening Dyer had been roused from his armchair by the sound of a large cart being driven across the heath at speed, pulled by two heavy horses. Twice it had encircled his property before coming to a standstill outside the gate of his small cottage garden. When Dyer opened his curtains he saw a vision from Hell; illuminated by the wild streaks of lightning that were criss-crossing the open heathland and seemingly oblivious to the maelstrom around him, the driver sat atop the cart – Jed Stephens's eyes were wide open and his left arm was pointing reproachfully towards the terrified minister.

"Dyer had watched as the cart took off once more, believing that it was about to do a further lap of the cottage. Hastily grabbing his hat and bible, he ran from the house, leaping the small picket fence and following the well-worn path towards the village. He arrived at the *White Hart* in the manner I have previously described to you."

"A most remarkable account – and one that clearly struck some fear into the others," I ventured.

"Yes. The terror within the group was palpable. And the tension was further exacerbated with what happened next. We had no sooner succeeded in calming Dyer down, to a point where he could explain what had driven him from his home, when there was an almighty clamour on the main highway outside the inn. Through the line of small windows, we watched as the farm cart the minister had described earlier passed before us, the driver performing the same pointing ritual as he had done previously. Dyer immediately passed out and slumped to the floor. The others looked helplessly at each other, one or two mouthing that the driver had indeed been Stephens, the dead prize-fighter."

By now, I was thoroughly gripped by Holmes's narrative and the great detective was relishing the chance to play storyteller. I resisted the urge to interrupt, allowing him to go on.

"The locals were wild with excitement and it once again fell to me to take charge. I asked for volunteers to accompany me out into the storm to investigate. To a man, they looked at me in disbelief, before one of their number - a miller by the name of Charlie Stubbins - reluctantly agreed to don his cape and hat and venture from the inn.

"It was approaching half-past eleven as we trudged out into the darkness carrying a couple of lanterns provided by the landlord. The worst of the wind and rain appeared to have passed over, and we could hear but a faint rumble of thunder and see just the odd flash in the sky as the storm clouds headed out over the coast. Stubbins seemed bewildered by the fact that I had chosen not to follow the route of the farm cart, but had asked him instead to direct me towards the graveyard of the Methodist chapel. When we arrived at the scattering of gravestones alongside the austere Wesleyan building, he pointed out where Elizabeth Dyer had been buried. A cursory glance told me all that I needed to know – her grave showed no sign of having been disturbed."

I was a little puzzled by my friend's line of enquiry. "Why did you think that the daughter's grave might be disturbed? Her father had not mentioned seeing her."

Holmes replied without conceit: "I was merely eliminating the possibilities. I did not think for a moment that the body of

Elizabeth Dyer would play a part in this affair, but needed to be sure. Having done so, we then turned our attention to the grave of Jed Stephens, which lay only a few feet away. Stubbins took one look and declared with some surprise that the plot again looked undisturbed. I asked him to stand back from the grave and proceeded to carry out a thorough examination of the soil towards the head of the grave and some of the tell-tale signs on the muddy path leading to the newer burials. Having done so, I reached a different conclusion to the miller."

"Ah, ha! So you saw signs that the grave had been tampered with? I know that you would have been unlikely to believe that Stephens had come back from the dead, so I'm guessing that you were then working on the assumption that grave-robbers had been at work. Bodysnatching used to be very common in that part of East Anglia in days gone by."

"I assumed nothing, Watson. But it was clear that a body had been disinterred. There were two sets of footprints around the head of the grave and clear indentations where a wooden shovel had been inserted into the ground to locate the lid of the coffin."

"A wooden shovel?"

"Yes, a traditional metal spade is too noisy for men who wish to operate under the cover of darkness. The resurrectionists used a wooden shovel to remove the fresh, uncompacted, soil from the head of the grave, leaving the rest of the plot covered. With some skill, they then prised open the lid of the coffin and lifted it against the weight of the soil to enable the body to be pulled out head first. The grass nearby showed where they had placed the cadaver, before trying to tidy up and leave no trace of the exhumation – not an easy thing to achieve on an exceptionally wet night. They had then carried the body to the farm cart which had been left at the gates of the chapel. The wheel marks were still visible when we arrived."

I had to express some confusion. "You will forgive me, Holmes, but I thought that the horrors of the 'Resurrection Era' were behind us? There is no profit motive these days in stealing bodies to sell to unscrupulous surgeons. The *Anatomy Act* of 1832 did away with the nefarious trade by providing for a legitimate supply of bodies for anatomical dissection."

"You are quite correct, my friend. I followed the same line of reasoning and had to conclude that Stephens's body had been removed for an entirely different purpose. One that was to become clearer as the night went on. Having concluded our business at the graveyard, I then directed Stubbins to take me to the home of the village blacksmith."

"The blacksmith?"

"Yes, who better in that small, tight-knit, community to know who owned the farm cart we had seen. It took us three attempts to wake the aged forge master from his slumbers. He was none too pleased to be roused from his warm bed, but provided the crucial information we needed. The cart was used on a smallholding that belonged to the local surgeon, Dr Buckingham."

"How extraordinary! What possible motive could he have had for wanting to disinter the body? And why would he have wanted to pretend that the prize-fighter had come back from the dead?"

"These are key questions. And in due course, we had an answer to both. But first I had to carry out a little surreptitious task of my own. I instructed Stubbins to go to the home of Dr Buckingham and to tell him that a wealthy guest at the *White Hart* had been taken ill and required immediate attention. I then made my way back to the inn to await the arrival of the surgeon.

"It was some time before the medical man graced us with his presence. In the time before his arrival, I was able to reassure those that remained at the inn that there was a perfectly rational explanation for what they had witnessed earlier that evening. Evan Dyer looked unconvinced, still ranting that this was the work of supernatural forces. A little after one o'clock in the morning, Dr Buckingham knocked on the door of the *White Hart* and was shown in by the seemingly grateful landlord. He was led across to where I sat in a rocking chair close by the fire, covered in a large tartan blanket. The other men had positioned themselves out of sight, but within earshot, in a small room just off the main bar. They were as keen as I was to hear what the surgeon had to say.

"As Buckingham approached me, I looked up and beckoned for him to sit on a chair before the fire. He looked confused, but complied, setting down both his brown derby hat and black medical bag on the floor beside him. He was a stocky man, well over six feet in height, and some fifty years of age. While dark-haired, his long side-whiskers were flecked with grey. He spoke in a deep, confident tone: 'How may I be of assistance, Sir?'

"I now had him at my will and dispensed with the charade. 'Dr Buckingham. My name is Sherlock Holmes and I am a private consulting detective. I would be grateful if you could explain to me why you hired two body snatchers to dig up the grave of Jed Stephens earlier this evening and why you felt it necessary to commission them to parade his body around the village on your farm cart in order to strike terror into the heart of the Methodist minister, Evan Dyer.'

"Buckingham's composure did not falter. For some seconds he continued to stare at me, his keen eyes seeking further explanation for this unexpected challenge to his assumed authority. When at last he replied, it was with a wry smile. "My good Sir, it is not often that I am outwitted by anyone in this village. I confess to having no knowledge of what a *consulting detective* does, but imagine that you hail from somewhere other than Blythburgh. Either way, I am level-headed enough to recognise that you hold all of the cards in this particular play.'

"I thanked him for his candour and then threw down a further challenge. 'Would I be right in suggesting that your primary reason for wanting to dig up the dead body was professional pride? I believe you were keen to re-examine the arterial surgery you had carried out on Stephen's upper thigh to determine whether it was your own failed surgery that had led to his death, rather than the suggested infection. You would have had no opportunity to do that earlier as medical protocol dictated that an independent doctor should carry out the *post-mortem*.'

"For the first time, his eyes flickered, revealing that I had come close to the truth. 'How could you possibly know that? I have told no one about my reason for wanting to re-examine the cadaver. The two men I hired to exhume the body believed only that I wished to play an elaborate prank on Dyer, that infernal meddler and soap-box preacher. I was content for them to go through with the plan to strap the body to the seat of the cart and to control its movement by means of some poles and thin rope. They were positioned in the back of the cart so as not to be seen. I had suggested only that they should stop at Dyer's cottage on their way to my property. They took it upon themselves to pursue him through the village.'

"I then explained my reasoning: 'It was clear that there could be no profit motive in taking the body. Had that been the case, you would have asked for the cadaver of Elizabeth Dyer to be exhumed at the same time. You had no reason to do that, for you knew for certain what had led to her death. The only explanation that fitted the facts was the issue of your professional reputation – you had to be certain that your surgery had not been the cause of death.'

"Buckingham did not deny the truth of anything I had said. He went on to explain that his two accomplices were brothers, whose grandfather, Thomas Vaughan, had been a prolific East Anglian grave-robber decades before. They had used the tools of his trade to dig up Jed Stephens for a nominal sum. When the doctor had carried out his autopsy, they were to have returned his body to the graveyard. Beyond that, he believed that the men had done little wrong.

"I was quick to challenge this latter statement, taking the opportunity at that point to invite the locals back into the bar. What followed was a near brawl in which I feared that our medical man might indeed be lynched. But such was the persuasive influence of alcohol, that having paid the landlord to provide the men with whatever refreshments they desired, the doctor was able to convince the mob that his execution would be inadvisable. Most easily converted was the melancholy Methodist himself, who seemed only too happy to accept a bottle of cheap brandy as recompense for the distress he had suffered. By the early hours of the morning, all grievances had been settled and the weary men headed home to their beds."

I chuckled at the humour of it all. "A successful conclusion then?"

Holmes nodded and rose from his armchair. "Yes. And I think further drinks are in order – spirits of a very different kind."

# 3. The Manila Envelope

When Mr Lionel Longford had been seated in our study on a somewhat chilly evening in the late-April of 1882, I was inclined to believe that his very dull tale about receiving a letter bearing a collectable postage stamp would be of little interest to my busy detective colleague. And yet, from the off, Holmes had sat forward in his armchair listening intently to every syllable uttered by the fair-haired ledger clerk.

The preamble was as straightforward as Mr Longford appeared to be. The thin, hollow-cheeked fellow told us that he was thirty-two years of age and worked for the Clerkenwell firm of Charlton, Peabody & Snell. He was unmarried and lived with an older sister in a two-storey mid-terrace house on the Farringdon Road. Alongside his enjoyment of accordion music, Longford's main hobby in life was to collect postage stamps, of which he had amassed over 300 since starting the collection ten years earlier.

I have no doubt that Longford would have regaled us with a detailed account of each and every stamp in his possession had Holmes not intervened at the critical juncture. "Mr Longford, your fascination for philately is clear, but I wonder if you would be kind enough to tell us all about the envelope you received this morning which has prompted your visit here this evening."

Longford looked stunned and slightly embarrassed by Holmes's remark and piped up immediately. "Mr Holmes, until this morning I had not known about you, or your work. But one of my work colleagues, Elijah Rendle, explained that you would be the man to consult about this very curious matter. I must apologise, for I had not realised that he had already contacted you about the envelope."

Holmes smiled and shook his head. "To my knowledge, I have never had any communication with your Mr Rendle. My work requires me to make rational deductions based on the facts presented and any additional information I am able to observe. It was a simple matter to determine why you came to see me."

Longford shifted uneasily in the chair. "Well, you have the better of me, Mr Holmes..."

I could not help intervening at this point, for I was becoming more accustomed to Holmes's methods and fancied that I could shed some light on the matter. "Mr Longford. I am sure that my colleague will forgive the interruption, but there is no great mystery in this. Your attire attests to your stated profession: a smart frock coat and necktie; patent black leather shoes; a tailor-made waistcoat; and a new bowler. That you have been at work today is obvious from the ink stains on your hands and left shirt cuff. Given the time that you arrived, I would say that you left work at five-thirty and took the decision to come to Baker Street at that point. Had you planned the visit earlier, I feel certain your professional approach would have been to send a telegram ahead of your arrival. That this is a matter of some concern is apparent from the nervousness which you have displayed since entering the room. And the object of your uneasiness must be the envelope which is protruding from the outside pocket of your coat; whether you were aware of it or not, you have checked for its presence at least three or four times since being seated. Now, having told us about your long-standing pastime, I am inclined to believe that it was the postage stamp on this envelope which first caught your attention."

"Bravo, Watson!" said Holmes, "A fine hypothesis." He looked towards our guest. "Now then, Mr Longford, is Dr Watson correct? Was it indeed the stamp which first struck you as odd?"

Longford now looked more confused than ever, but reached to his side and withdrew the envelope. He passed it to me, before adding, "See for yourself, Doctor. Is it not curious?"

I scanned the envelope quickly - noting only that the name and address were handwritten in black ink - and then focused my attention on the stamp at its corner. A small, perforated, rose-coloured stamp printed on white paper, across one edge of which was a smudged postmark bearing the word 'Islington'. I had to confess to seeing nothing curious at all, and passed the envelope across to Holmes as Longford indicated the nature of his concern.

"It's the denomination, you see. A five shilling stamp newly printed this year - although the design is a re-issue of one that was used up until 1878. An envelope of this weight could have been posted in London for as little as a penny, so why did the sender use such a high denomination stamp?"

Holmes sat upright and began to scrutinise every aspect of the envelope. "Why indeed?" he replied. "Now, tell me, Mr Longford. Beyond the stamp, what is it that really concerns you?"

"Well, I received the envelope in the first post this morning, as I was about to set off for work. I wasn't expecting any letters and rarely correspond with anyone. I have no friends outside of work, both my parents are dead and my only other relative is my sister, Leticia. I was first struck by the stamp, but having opened the envelope when I first arrived at work, realised - as I see you have now done – that it contains no letter, card or other contents. It is essentially just an envelope sent with an expensive stamp."

"And this worried you sufficiently to discuss the matter first with Mr Rendle, and, at his suggestion, to bring the envelope to me?"

Once again, our guest looked somewhat uncomfortable. "Yes, I am easily unnerved by anything out of the ordinary and have a predictable pattern of life where everything must have its place. I do not keep abreast of anything that is happening in the wider world, for fear that my life is about to be upturned. So, as you might imagine, I was greatly disturbed by the envelope, although I realise now that this may look like a very trivial affair to you, Mr Holmes."

To my great surprise, Holmes answered in the negative. "On the contrary, Mr Longford, I believe this to be anything other than trivial. Furthermore, it is a matter which I am very happy to look into. I have one immediate question for you, though – why did you assume that this was addressed to you and not your sister?" He pointed to the front of the envelope. "It merely says, 'L Longford'."

"That is a fair question, but Leticia is even less likely than I to receive letters. Her husband died three years ago, leaving her with little money. In order to pay the rent, she was forced to accept a lodger and makes a meagre living taking in washing and ironing for other folk. She rarely leaves the house other than to buy groceries and other provisions and has no friends that I know of. I cannot recollect that she has ever received a letter."

I was struck by a sudden thought. "Is it possible that the envelope was sent to you by someone who knows of your collecting hobby? If the high denomination stamp was a gift, the sender may not have intended to send an accompanying letter."

Longford was very clear in his response. "No. Only my sister knows of my hobby. I have not even told anyone at work. I have occasionally taken used stamps from the envelopes of business letters where these have been placed in the wastepaper basket. While there is no harm in this, I would feel uncomfortable if my colleagues knew."

Holmes then continued. "Unfortunately, there is little that we can ascertain about the sender from this envelope beyond his being a well-educated, left-handed inmate of Pentonville prison who is currently awaiting trial."

Longford and I were both taken aback. "How did you gather all of that from an empty envelope?" our guest asked.

"Our sender has written the name and address extremely neatly with a nib pen, and in a flowing style without errors or hesitation. All of this suggests a man who has enjoyed a good education. That he is left-handed is also clear. There is no disguising the occasional smudging as the writing hand has moved across the ink before it has dried fully.

"That he has access to a nib pen and ink makes me believe he is awaiting trial rather than already serving a sentence. In recent years, I have corresponded with a number of prison inmates. Invariably, their letters are written in pencil as they are not allowed the luxury of a steel pen. Since 1877, when all prisons came under the control of our national government, prisoners on remand and those awaiting trial have been afforded much more freedom to write letters, principally to allow them to correspond with their legal representatives. In general, they are allowed one letter per day, which is paid for by the government. Beyond that, a prisoner must pay for the postage of any additional letters. I believe that has happened here.

"If we turn to the envelope itself, there are further tell-tale signs that this has been sent from a prison. The inexpensive manila envelope is now standard issue in many institutions, as is this type of cheap black ink. That this has come from a place of correction is confirmed also by the faint whiff of oakum on the paper – a sure sign that our sender has been engaged in the laborious and mind-numbing task of unpicking tarred naval rope. This is an activity which most new arrivals at prison are required to perform for at least the first nine months of their incarceration.

"Finally, as the postmark reads 'Islington' - which denotes the Northern District Branch Office of the Royal Mail - we can safely deduce that our prison is Pentonville, which sits on the Caledonian Road in the Barnsbury area."

Longford looked incredulous. "That is remarkable, Mr Holmes! But why was a five shilling stamp used rather than a cheaper alternative?"

Holmes seemed pleased that the question had been asked. "You will understand that any form of currency is in short supply within a prison. With an absence of cash, any commodity can become a form of tender. Typically, prisoners and unscrupulous prison officers will trade in tobacco and cigarettes, but stamps would serve equally well. Our sender would have used any source to obtain a stamp and I believe that the denomination was largely irrelevant. He was willing to pay any price just to send the envelope."

"So would it have been inspected by the prison authorities before it was sent?"

"Yes. The governor or deputy governor would check any envelopes or parcels that are sent or received. They would ensure that prisoners had not infringed any rules and would censor any complaints about the prison and its regime."

This time, it was I who asked: "Is it possible then, that a letter might have been removed from the envelope by the prison authorities?"

"It is possible, but unlikely in this case. I believe that our man wished to send this envelope exactly as you see it. Its real message is hidden you see, so that only the recipient would be able to read it."

Once again, Longford looked baffled. "I'm afraid that I do not see, Sir."

"Then you will have to trust me with what I am about to do to the envelope in a short while. Before we get to that, I have a few more questions."

"Certainly - I will be pleased to oblige."

"How long have you been living with your sister?"

"I moved in three weeks ago, when Lawrence Carpenter moved out."

"Would this be the lodger you referred to earlier?"

"Yes, my sister said he had accepted a position on a merchant ship destined for South Africa. In the time that he had lived at Farringdon Road, he had always spent weeks away, travelling here and there, but this was to be a permanent move. She said they had parted on good terms. I agreed to move in to help her with the loss of income."

"And when the envelope was delivered this morning, did your sister know that you had picked it up and taken it to work?"

Longford seemed bemused by the question. "No. She had left the house early to collect some washing from one of her regular customers. I was eager to get to work and left before she returned. And coming here as I have since finishing work, I have not seen her since."

Holmes sat forward in his chair once again. "I see. Tell me more about this lodger, Lawrence Carpenter."

"A sea-faring man, as I have said. Tall, ginger-haired and well-spoken. I met him on a few occasions when I visited my sister. We had a shared interest in accountancy. I was pleasantly surprised to learn that he was a ship's bursar and very good with numbers. He had originally replied to an advertisement which my sister had placed in the window of a baker's shop. She believed him to be a sober and trustworthy character and agreed to let him lodge in the spare room at the back of the house. He proved to be an exemplary lodger, always paying his rent on time and keeping his room clean and tidy. Beyond that, I can tell you no more."

Holmes nodded. "That is most informative, Mr Longford. Now I will leave you in Dr Watson's capable hands for just a few short minutes and feel confident that when I return I will be able to shed more light on this curious affair."

With no further explanation, Holmes leapt up from his chair and headed out of the room. I heard his footfall on the stairs, yet did not hear him exit the front door. In his absence, I asked Longford more about his stamp collecting, a ruse that I knew would compel the man to talk and break the silence until my colleague returned.

A good ten minutes had elapsed before Holmes once more ascended the stairs and returned to the study. His face was radiant as he entered the room and addressed our guest. "I must apologise for the time it has taken me to complete such a simple task. I inadvertently interrupted one of Mrs Hudson's baking sessions and was scolded for wanting to commandeer the use of her kettle. In short, I have steamed the five shilling stamp from the envelope. I imagine you will want to keep this for your collection?"

Longford took the stamp presented to him and looked up at Holmes. "That is very kind of you, but I could easily have removed the stamp myself when I got home."

Holmes chuckled. "You misunderstand my actions. I removed the stamp because I believed there would be a message hidden beneath it. It was the only place on the envelope that could not be viewed by the prison authorities."

I could tell that Holmes's supposition had proved to be correct. "So, what is this hidden message?"

"It is written in ink, in the smallest of handwriting, and appears to be a very cryptic communication. It reads: '*One ate for free, oh, none for tea.*'"

It was my turn to chortle. "And do you have any idea what it means?"

"Of course, it is not so complicated. But before I explain, I must just check something."

He was once again out of his chair, this time rummaging around on the floor, sifting through a considerable pile of discarded newspapers and hastily reading sections of the broadsheets he had chosen to select. Minutes later, he exclaimed with some joy, "I have found it, my friends! I have found our man!"

Longford looked towards me for some sort of explanation, before Holmes continued. "I knew that the name Lawrence Carpenter sounded familiar. I have been checking the recent crime reports in *The Times*. It seems that a ship's bursar of that name has recently been charged with stealing a strongbox containing a considerable sum of money. While the shipping company and police believe they have a solid case against the man, the reports suggest that the strongbox has yet to be recovered. Without it, the defence believes that the case against Carpenter is purely circumstantial. Since being detained within Pentonville and awaiting his trial, all of Carpenter's communications have been monitored for clues as to the location of the stolen box."

The colour seemed to drain from Longford's face as he listened to this. "Oh, my word! I had no idea, Mr Holmes! But why would Carpenter want to send me this message? I can assure you that I had nothing to do with him or this crime!"

Holmes did not reply, but looked at Longford, smiled thinly and then raised his eyebrows. It did not take our guest too long to work it out for himself. "This is worse than I thought, Sir! Are you saying that Carpenter's message was intended for Leticia – she was the 'L Longford' it was addressed to?"

"It is the only explanation which fits the facts, so let me paint you a picture. Is it so hard to imagine, that in the void left by the death of her husband, your sister would fall in love with the man she had taken in as a lodger? And in seeking to secure their future together, the ship's bursar hatches a plan to steal a sizeable sum of money. Whether she knew from the start, or whether he was forced to confide in her later, Carpenter tells Leticia where the strongbox is hidden. When his crime is discovered, he denies all, having secreted away the crucial evidence and remaining confident that he will be acquitted of any charge brought against him.

"In playing her part, Leticia says nothing to the police, maintaining that she knew little about what her lodger had been up to. The police search her home and find no strongbox, so naturally assume her to be telling the truth. She accounts for Carpenter's departure by telling you the tale about his planned move to South Africa. She is confident that you will not have read about his crime as you have no interest in current affairs. You readily agree to move in with her, easing some of the burden she must now feel."

"I do not like the thought that Leticia has deceived me in such a way, but cannot deny that she has been acting out of character recently. It is wholly possible that she has fallen for Carpenter's charms and could not tell me of his scheme. But I am still not sure what this cryptic message is. What was he trying to tell her?"

Holmes repeated the words. "'One ate for free, oh, none for tea' is confirmation of her complicity in this crime. Carpenter is telling her the coded number sequence for unlocking the strongbox. It has a combination lock similar to that invented four years ago by the German, Joseph Loch. His innovative mechanism was first used by Tiffany's Jewellers in New York. Without the correct combination of numbers, it would be impossible to open the box without heavy cutting equipment. Leticia could not risk trying to move the box from its secret location, but with the code could open it and remove the money."

I was fascinated to hear this, but, like Longford, could still not see how the message revealed any numbers. Holmes then explained: 'One ate for free' is simply the numbers, *1, 8, 4* and *3*. The second part of the message is more convoluted, but still identifies the remaining four digits. 'Oh' and 'none' both hint at *zero*, while 'for tea' is clearly *40* or *4* and *0*. The coded combination is therefore *18430040*."

"Amazing," said Longford, "but where does that leave Leticia and I? I suppose you are forced to go to the authorities with this information, Mr Holmes. It seems I have unwittingly placed my sister in quite a predicament."

My colleague gave a considered reply. "That is very much up to you. I suggest you take the envelope and explain to your sister that you know what has occurred. Then ask what she thinks is best. I cannot answer for your conscience or hers, but imagine that the authorities would look more favourably on Leticia's role within all of this, if she were to disclose where the stolen strongbox is located. This is really a test of how much affection and loyalty she has towards Lawrence Carpenter. Is it a bond for which she is prepared to risk a lengthy prison sentence?"

The question hung in the air as the ledger clerk considered what Holmes had said. A few seconds later he looked up, smiled weakly and then said, "I must pay you for your time. It was remiss of me, dealing with money as I do every day, not to have asked you at the start what your fee would be."

"There is nothing to pay," was the reply. "I ask only that you let us know what you decide to do. And I would be grateful if you could desist from letting the police know of our involvement in this matter. It would not do for Scotland Yard to think that I had withheld crucial evidence in a major criminal trial."

"Thank you, Mr Holmes. You have my word that I will say nothing about your role here today."

*********************

As a medical man, I realised very early in my career that there is often no certainty or predictability about the way that individuals will decide to act in moments of extreme tension or crisis. When I was later to serve in the army, I saw tangible evidence of this on a daily basis. So it was, that having believed Leticia Longford would respond to the pleas of her younger brother and go to the police with the envelope from Lawrence Carpenter, I was to learn two days later that she had resisted all attempts to persuade her to take the obvious course of action.

I had just returned to 221B after a morning spent at my tailor's being fitted for a new brushed cotton sack coat, to find Holmes in a solemn mood.

"You have just missed Mr Longford," he announced, looking thoughtfully towards his violin which lay with its bow on the table before him. "He was most distraught. Having taken the envelope to his sister, he confided that he knew all about Carpenter, the stolen strongbox and the combination code. She was stunned and furious that he had intercepted the message. Despite his views on the matter, it seems that she believed she could still outwit the authorities.

"After their argument, she left the house and went straight to the allotment shed where Carpenter had apparently hidden the box. She did not, of course, realise that two Scotland Yard detectives had been watching the house, waiting to see if the envelope – which they knew had been delivered to the Farringdon Road address - might prompt such an action. She was duly arrested in possession of a large sum of money and later charged with assisting in the robbery. I have no doubt that like Carpenter she will face a considerable custodial sentence when brought to trial."

"And what of Lionel Longford?" I asked. "Is he likely to face any charges?"

"No. His sister has been tight-lipped on his behalf, claiming that she took delivery of the envelope and her brother had nothing to do with the affair."

"A very sorry business, Holmes."

"Yes," he replied. "Rational deduction does not always allow us to understand the vagaries of cognitive decision making. Where matters of the heart are concerned it seems that reason and judiciousness are discarded far too easily."

I could not disagree, but smiled inwardly, recognising that he rarely understood the lengths that some people would go to for love.

\*\*\*\*\*\*\*\*\*\*\*\*\*\*\*\*\*\*\*\*\*\*\*

There was one further postscript to this case which is worthy of mention. A week after Leticia Longford was tried at the Old Bailey and sentenced to five years in prison for her part in the strongbox robbery we received an unexpected visitor at Baker Street. Inspector Bradstreet of Scotland Yard's 'E' Division called that particular afternoon and asked to see Holmes.

The tall and wily officer could not suppress a grin as he asked whether my colleague had seen the outcome of the Carpenter/Longford case. Holmes played him with a straight bat: "Yes, of course, my dear Inspector. And a very good result for the Yard, I must admit."

Bradstreet was not to be outdone. "Mr Holmes, you might like to know that a key part of our success in bringing these felons to justice was a very vital clue. Carpenter sent a coded message from his Pentonville cell to the address of his beloved accomplice. We know this because we followed the said envelope on every part of its journey. In fact, for a while, we believed that Leticia Longford's brother, Lionel, was the intended recipient and followed him to work the day the envelope was delivered."

"I see," said Holmes, doing his best to maintain his composure.

"Yes. The strange thing was that when my men trailed him on his homeward journey, he took an unexpected detour. A detour which, I have to say, threw the two detectives completely. Having been walking through Clerkenwell in the direction of his home, he stopped suddenly and decided to hail a cab. The hansom took off in a completely different direction leaving my men temporarily flummoxed. When they were able to requisition a cab of their own, they managed to follow Longford as far as Euston Road, but then lost sight of his hansom in the heavy traffic around Regent's Park."

Looking somewhat relieved, Holmes then ventured: "That is unfortunate, Bradstreet. Still, it must have been some reassurance to learn later that Mr Longford had nothing to do with the crime?"

Bradstreet gave him a steely gaze and set his teeth hard. "Indeed. Otherwise, we have another mystery on our hands."

"And what mystery is that?" I asked.

"The mystery surrounding the address which my detectives thought they heard Longford give to the cabbie when he first hailed that hansom. They could not be sure – against the hubbub of noise on Calthorpe Street - but fancied that they heard the words, '221B Baker Street'."

Holmes snorted. "Now that is indeed a mystery – and one which we are unlikely to get to the bottom of."

"I feared as much," was all that Bradstreet could add.

# 4. The Radicant Munificent Society

It was in the year 1889 that Mr Sherlock Holmes was engaged in one of the most lucrative cases of his long and eventful career. And like so many of our colourful adventures together, it began with a light breeze, which only hinted at the gathering storm that was about to engulf us.

"That really does not bode well, Watson," said Holmes peering skywards through the window of the Baker Street apartment. "The wind is picking up and there is a distinct weather front closing in with very heavy rainclouds. And do you know what day it is?"

I looked up from the *Daily Telegraph.* "Indeed, I do – the fifteenth of July, *St Swithun's Day.* And according to English folklore, rain today will lead inexorably to inclement weather for the next forty days."

"What a fanciful notion! When have you ever known me to pay any heed to pagan or religious superstition? The day I was referring to, is the third Monday in July, the day traditionally set aside for the annual gathering of the Radicant Munificent Society.

"Well, I've never heard of such an organisation," I said gruffly.

Holmes smirked. "That may be because the society generally keeps its events and activities hidden, away from public scrutiny. It is an ancient order, dedicated primarily to clandestine meetings and underhand dealings. First set up with the patronage of King Henry I's daughter, Matilda – the

Empress Maud – who led a bloody military campaign against the rule of Stephen of Blois, the king's nephew, who assumed the throne in 1135."

"And what does this ancient society do in these more enlightened times?"

"Their original mission was to undermine the existence of the Jewish moneylenders whom they believed were financing King Stephen's reign. And while they shunned the use of violence, they used their considerable legal and monetary skills to perpetrate fraud, embezzlement and counterfeiting to destabilise the fiscal affairs of the king. Theirs was a membership which grew steadily by word of mouth and personal introductions, from an initial cohort of six agents to a secret society of several hundred. The name 'Radicant' derives from this approach of *bringing forth roots* – their motto - although it was coined much later, in the mid-part of the eighteenth century, by its young president at that time, the Scottish philosopher Adam Smith."

"And the 'Munificent' bit? I asked. "Surely the organisation cannot claim to be pursuing benevolent or charitable aims?"

"Again, an eighteenth century affectation. By that stage, the 'Radicant Brotherhood' had transformed itself into a gentlemen's club which operated purely to further the financial interests of its members, each helping the other to rise within the ranks of their chosen legal or financial profession. But mindful of the sometimes hostile public reaction to their covert activities, Adam Smith persuaded the society to change its name and to establish a charitable wing. To that end, the Radicant Munificent Society restricted its membership to a maximum of twenty-five, and required each member to contribute to a separate endowment fund from which money could be distributed annually to impoverished families in the East End of London. The day chosen for the distribution of their *penny bundles* is the third Monday in July each year. It prompts a carnival-like procession, which I suspect will be severely dampened this afternoon by the arrival of these enormous storm clouds." With that, Holmes turned from the window and took his seat in the armchair close to the fireplace. I noted that he held within one hand what looked like a telegram.

"I see, but why is it that you take such an interest in their affairs?" I asked, still unsure why Holmes had raised the matter.

"Very straightforward - each member of the society is honour-bound to attend the ceremony in their colourful regalia and in the full glare of the press and public. It is the one opportunity that outsiders may have to see who its members are. And I fancy that I will attend this year, to see if I can get a clear view of their new president, Mr Morley Merrill-Adams."

"The name means nothing to me, Holmes."

"No, but if I were to tell you that the gentleman concerned masquerades as the head of a major joint-stock bank, while at the same time operating as the chief accountant for a major ring of gem and bullion thieves, you will understand my interest. His criminal accomplices have been specifically targeting the businesses of wealthy Jewish goldsmiths and diamond dealers in the Hatton Garden area of Holborn. His rise to power within the society is a clear sign that the ancient order is refocusing its efforts on its anti-Semitic roots."

"And is he dangerous, this Merrill-Adams?"

"That remains to be seen. We will be joined in a few moments by a Mr Samuel Mendoza who has asked me to look into the affairs of the Radicant Munificent Society," said

Holmes, waving the telegram as the clock on the mantelpiece gently chimed out the hour of ten o'clock. "He believes that it is planning to promulgate a campaign of anti-Jewish activity in the heart of the East End."

No sooner had he said this, when there was a ring on the doorbell below us. We heard Mrs Hudson answer the door and direct our guest up the stairs to the first floor room. Holmes sprang into action, opening the door at the loud knock, introducing the two of us and beckoning for Mr Mendoza to be seated.

Samuel Mendoza cut a striking figure. He wore an expensively-tailored dark blue frock coat with matching trousers and waistcoat and carried within his hand a gold-topped cane. He was of average height - perhaps five feet, seven inches tall – with a handsome, lean face, chestnut brown eyes and short, raven-coloured hair. While slight, he was powerfully built, with strong upper arms and sturdy legs. Above one eye he was sporting a distinct cut, about two inches long, which was still markedly swollen.

I watched Holmes study Mendoza carefully as our guest took a seat opposite him near the fireplace.

"The likeness is remarkable, Mr Mendoza, and I am sure that your great great grandfather, Daniel, would be pleased to know that you still carry on the family tradition of boxing."

Mendoza's thick fingers moved instinctively towards the abrasion above his eyebrow before returning to the pocket of his waistcoat. "Is it really that obvious?" he replied, looking distinctly uncomfortable. "And how did you know he was my relative?"

"Dan Mendoza is a sporting hero of mine," replied Holmes, with obvious enthusiasm. "A Whitechapel man of Portuguese-

Jewish descent, who fought hard to become English boxing champion for the three years from 1792. Unlike the heavyweight sloggers of his generation, Dan was a gifted pugilist and a supreme tactician. He outwitted many of his heavier rivals by his clever and defensive moves – ducking, diving, blocking and side-stepping – in what others have called the *scientific style*. I have a treasured copy of his 1789 book, *The Art of Boxing* on the bookshelf behind you. There is no mistaking the likeness – I also possess a rare etching of the man produced at the time. He had to be one of your forebears. And given your age and the passing of years, it seemed most likely that he was your great great grandfather."

"That is incredible, Mr Holmes. Your services come highly recommended. I can already see why."

"A mere trifle. Now, do not let me delay you in the main aim of your visit here today. Dr Watson is a respected colleague who undertakes investigations alongside me, very much as an equal partner. You can be frank in telling us the nature of your concerns about the Radicant Munificent Society."

I felt myself blush at Holmes's words. I had, to that point, always viewed myself as a supportive friend, a chronicler and, to some extent, an unofficial biographer, but his allusion to some sort of parity of esteem was indeed flattering.

Mendoza sat forward in the armchair and began his narrative. "You are correct, Mr Holmes, in that I do still choose to box, as four generations of my family have done before me. These days it is purely a leisurely pursuit. We come from a long and distinguished line of Sephardic Jews who settled, finally, in the East End of London and have, since that time, built a very good jewellery business in Hatton Garden. My family and I worship at a synagogue in Aldgate and I play an active role in the life of our community. A community which is now under threat from the society you referred to."

I thought it striking that Mendoza appeared to be reluctant to mention the name of the organisation. The deep hatred he had for it soon became apparent.

"My first knowledge of this secret society came through a chance encounter with Mr Morley Merrill-Adams, who is now its president. Some six months ago our family business needed assistance. Our bankers to that point - while proficient and obliging - were just not big enough to support our growing need for investment capital on a host of new ventures. We are expanding our operations at a rapid pace and needed banking advisors up to the task. We parted company with the bank on mutually friendly terms and looked around for an alternative. The name Pendleton-Lyons was suggested to us and I arranged a meeting with its head banker, Morley Merrill-Adams.

"From the moment I was introduced to him, it was clear that Merrill-Adams had an animosity towards my people. I have encountered all sorts of enmity towards Jews as I have lived and worked in this country, but rarely have I known a man of such standing and reputation to be so hostile towards our very existence. He could barely look me in the eye and when I first shook his hand, I noted that he withdrew it quickly and then proceeded to wipe his palm with a handkerchief that he pulled from his pocket. At every point of enquiry, he announced that Pendleton-Lyons could be of no assistance. Within less than five minutes our meeting was concluded. He could apparently offer no help and we were no closer to finding a new banker. I was frustrated and as I rose to leave his office, he concluded by saying, 'There is no place for your kind in this great city of ours and I would not sully the reputation of this fine bank by taking you on as a client.

The name of the Radicant Munificent Society may mean nothing to you at the present time, but rest assured, within a few months it will. Watch your back, Mr Mendoza. And tell your family and friends to do the same.'

"As you might imagine, gentlemen, I was both shocked and enraged by this. Were it not for the restraint and control I have learnt through my boxing – qualities inherited, no doubt, from my famous ancestor - I would gladly have floored the man that instant, but held my head high and left the building without any further dialogue. Since then, we have appointed new bankers, but I have not been able to ignore the existence of the organisation he alluded to."

Holmes's face took on an expression of deep apprehension as he addressed our guest. "Your telegram mentioned some incidents in recent weeks which have given you a particular cause for concern?"

Mendoza nodded. "Yes, not long after my meeting with Merrill-Adams, we had bricks thrown through the windows of two of our shops and anti-Semitic slogans chalked on the brickwork nearby. Such incidents have occurred in the past, and I was not immediately concerned. Then, threatening letters began to be posted through the letterbox of my home and I learned later at the synagogue that other high-profile members of our community had been similarly targeted. On the back of this, in early-May, we had a significant robbery at one of the premises we use to cut, polish and store the diamonds of our trade. And it was not an isolated incident – since then, three other raids have taken place on Jewish-owned businesses in the Hatton Garden area. While Scotland Yard has investigated, no one has yet been brought to book for any of these crimes."

I took the opportunity to interject. "Mr Mendoza, I can imagine that these events are particularly alarming to you and your family. In fact, they are a concern to us all. But, without seeming impertinent, I am curious to know how you can be so certain that all of the incidents were perpetrated by the Radicant Munificent Society?"

Mendoza was not in the least ruffled by my polite challenge. "A fair question, Dr Watson. I had my suspicions, of course, when those windows were broken - one of the chalk messages said: 'You were warned'. And with the first robbery, I was convinced that the events were indeed being orchestrated by the same people. Yet there was little I could point to as proof. I did mention to Scotland Yard the earlier meeting with Merrill-Adams, but the inspector in charge of the investigations seemed content to play down the significance of the threat."

Holmes looked up again keenly. "I see. And what was the name of this Inspector?"

"Ridgeley."

"Alas, a name that is unfamiliar to me, Mr Mendoza. But please, carry on, you were about to tell us about the letter you received yesterday from your bankers announcing that they can no longer act for your business. Furthermore, you lost your dog while out walking this morning and now believe that it has been kidnapped. And on your journey here today you were dispossessed of a much-loved pocket watch."

The colour seemed to drain from Mendoza's face as he stared at my colleague in astonishment. He then cast a glance in my direction. Being used to such pronouncements my face remained impassive and when he turned back to Holmes and attempted to respond, his voice wavered momentarily. "I...I find myself at a loss to know how any man could possibly guess at such facts, Mr Holmes. It is just not possible..."

Holmes chuckled. "There is no guesswork involved, just the science of deduction, my life's work. Your telegram was sent yesterday evening. It summarised your concerns regarding the Radicant Munificent Society and hinted at the events of recent weeks. It then talked about 'pressing fiduciary matters'. I know something of Mr Merrill-Adams's form in undermining successful businesses. Coupled with what you told us earlier, it seemed likely that he was up to his old tricks in using his banking connections to put out the word that your business enterprise is not to be trusted and thereby prompting your new bankers to act. And as you appear to be a man who acts with some alacrity, it seemed safe to assume that you had received the letter the same day."

Mendoza looked on, spellbound, as Holmes continued: "There are visible black and white hairs on your trousers and the right-hand sleeve of your frockcoat. And yet you are immaculately turned out and prone, I would venture, to some fastidiousness. That you have had no opportunity to brush your clothing suggests that the hairs were picked up earlier this morning. Coupled with the distinct tooth marks on your elegant cane, this hints at a dog for which you have some affection and the lead and collar - still visible in your outer pocket - confirm the matter. The traces of red mud and brick dust on the sides of your boots lead me to believe that you were walking your dog close to some of the new building work on Saffron Hill. That it has gone missing is evident from the fact that you still carry the lead and collar. And yet, you would not have abandoned the beloved creature without a thorough search and a check to ensure that it had not returned home. Having done so, you could only have concluded that someone had taken the dog. A fear no doubt exacerbated by the other events of recent weeks."

"Truly remarkable, Mr Holmes. But my pocket watch can only have been taken in the last hour. I had to give up the fruitless search for young Bengal, my Newfoundland, to be certain of meeting you, as arranged, at this time. I checked the watch just before I hailed a cab on the Gray's Inn Road. And yet when I reached Baker Street, I realised that it had gone."

As Mendoza delivered the last few words, Holmes leapt from his chair and took up a position to the side of one of the curtains near the main window of the study. "Yes indeed, I watched you from this very window. It was the first action you took having paid the cabbie. Your hand went to the pocket of your waistcoat and I could see the discomfort on your face as you realised that the watch and its chain were missing - a treasured family heirloom, most likely once the property of your great great grandfather."

Mendoza again looked stunned. "You are not wrong. How did you know?"

"When I first mentioned your sporting ancestor, your hand went initially to the cut above your eyebrow and then to the pocket of your waistcoat - a clear indication that the timepiece had once belonged to Dan Mendoza. The pained expression again convinced me that the watch was missing. And it can only have been stolen while you ambled along the Gray's Inn Road. Taken no doubt by one of Merrill-Adams's henchmen."

"Is that likely? I queried.

"Oh yes. Merrill-Adams means to finish the task he has embarked upon. Your robber was no opportunist, Mr Mendoza. He was instructed to follow you and to find every opportunity to frustrate your movements, which would have included the theft of the dog. Tell me – as you were hailing the cab, do you remember seeing anyone else?"

Mendoza fell silent for a few seconds and then his face lit up. "Yes! Now I remember. It was busy and there were lots of people out walking. I stood on the kerb and waved as I saw a cab approaching. It took a short while to reach me. As I did so, a young fellow in a tweed jacket collided with me and nearly sent me tumbling. He was very apologetic and as I assured him that no harm had been done, the cab pulled up and I climbed in."

"A ruse," said Holmes. "And one that has given Merrill-Adams a head start on me."

"What do you mean, sir?"

"This young fellow you referred to. Was he also wearing a straw boater?"

"He was."

"In that case, the same man is now stood on the pavement opposite, facing 221B and doing a very poor job of pretending to read a newspaper. I fear it will be but a short time before he reports back to Merrill-Adams that the man he has been tailing has sought a consultation with London's only consulting detective - unless, of course, we can apprehend him first!"

With that, Holmes moved quickly from the window and turned to our guest. "Mr Mendoza, I require your assistance. I would like you to make your way back down the stairs and out on to the street. There you will make a very visible display of hailing the first cab that you see and engaging the cabbie in a lengthy enquiry. I am hoping that our watcher will linger for a while longer, curious to know what you are up to. In that time, Watson and I will do our best to confront him. Come, Watson, we leave by the back door!"

I had but a few seconds to grab a small cudgel that lay on a sideboard just inside the door. The three of us then took to the stairs, Holmes and I making for the rear of 221B. Some moments later, we had emerged onto a narrow passageway that ran towards Dorset Street. From there, it was a brisk trot back to Baker Street. We crossed the road and did our best to negotiate our way along the busy thoroughfare, walking at speed, but trying not to draw any particular attention to ourselves. Within twenty yards, Holmes turned to me quickly and whispered: "Up ahead, Watson, and he has his back to us!"

As we approached the man, I glanced across the road and saw that Mendoza had played his part. A hackney carriage stood outside 221B, its jarvey deep in conversation. Our quarry was watching attentively over the top of his raised newspaper, unaware that we were now upon him. Deftly, Holmes sidled up to the man and with his right hand snapped one half of a pair of handcuffs onto the left wrist of our prey. Startled, he dropped his newspaper and tried instinctively to pull his wrist away, but found that he was now attached to a grinning Sherlock Holmes. A look of anger flashed across his face and I could see that he was contemplating a resort to violence. I stepped around my colleague and brought the cudgel up into his view. His shoulders slumped instantly and his face took on a look of visible dejection.

"Now, who do we have here?" asked Holmes brightly. He stared directly at the fellow, who looked to be no older than nineteen or twenty. "There is no mistaking the ginger hair, thin nose and freckled face, Watson. And with a talent for pickpocketing, this has to be Curly Jamieson's lad, Ned."

The young lad smiled uneasily. "How'd you know 'bout me and my old man, mister? I ain't never seen you before."

Holmes laughed. "We may not have met, but you will have heard of me. I live across the street, in the house that you were watching. Sherlock Holmes is the name." Jamieson looked startled at the revelation and tried once again to pull his left wrist away from my colleague.

"Steady, young fellow!" I cautioned. "We have a few questions, so it would be in your best interests to calm down and accompany us across the street to the house in question."

Jamieson put up no further resistance. Holmes and I marched him across the street where we joined the waiting Mendoza. He merely nodded in confirmation that this was indeed the young chap who had collided with him earlier in the day. At Holmes's direction, I then paid the waiting driver for his time, explaining that his services were not needed after all.

When settled back in 221B, Holmes removed the handcuffs from our now timorous prisoner. "Just how is your father, Mr Jamieson? I should explain that I first met him five years ago, when he was still performing his magic tricks as part of a circus act. When that line of work dried up, he began to get more inventive with his hands, pickpocketing unsuspecting gentlemen in Kensington and Chelsea. I had no idea that his only son had gone into the same line."

Jamieson looked at him defiantly. "My father is the best at what he does. And what I do is my own affair. I knows you're some sort of clever clogs, but 'ave no idea why you've brought me 'ere."

Holmes dispensed with the pleasantries. "In that case, we'll get straight down to business." He pointed his open hand in the direction of Mendoza. "Firstly, I think you should return this gentleman's pocket watch. We know that you stole it earlier and I checked as we came up the stairs. You have it in the right outer pocket of your jacket."

Jamieson had little option but to comply. Mendoza looked greatly relieved as he was passed the watch and chain. Holmes then continued: "Now, perhaps you would be good enough to tell us where we might locate Mr Mendoza's missing Newfoundland puppy?"

The youngster looked a little more unsettled at the mention of the dog and tried to box clever. "Mr Holmes. Let's just say I do 'appen to know where the mutt is – 'ow much would that sort of information be worth?"

I could see that Mendoza was bristling, doing his best to maintain his composure - as was Holmes. My colleague's jaw was set hard as he continued: "Mr Jamieson. For the theft of the watch and the kidnapping of the animal, you could be looking at a seven-year stretch in Pentonville. Now, I'm taking it as read that the information about the dog will be forthcoming. Beyond that, if you wish to escape any charges in connection with your activities today, I suggest you tell us how you came to be working for Mr Morley Merrill-Adams."

The name was enough to provoke some alarm. Jamieson looked from Holmes towards Mendoza and then said quickly, "The dog was taken by a colleague of mine to my gaff in Clerkenwell. I live on Kirby Street - I can take you there, so no 'arm has been done. But I won't say nuffin' about Merrill-Adams. It's more than me life's worth."

"In that case, you will accompany Mr Mendoza to Kirby Street and if the dog is reunited with him – unharmed - I will do my best to protect you from any charges in connection with this affair." Mendoza was poised to raise an objection, but Holmes shot him a look and raised a finger, before continuing. "But I require one further piece of information from you – how many other 'colleagues' have been employed by Merrill-Adams to do the sort of work you have been engaged in?"

Jamieson was clearly more willing to talk about his criminal associates than he was his employer. "A dozen of us, all smart lads from the East End who have done time. I know a few of 'em and a couple are mighty handy with their fists."

I could tell by my colleague's fierce concentration that he had a clear line of enquiry. "Would I be right in assuming that you were all recruited by the same man?"

"Yeah. Merrill-Adams doesn't like to get his 'ands dirty. Has this sidekick – tall fella, with a long scar on his left cheek. Some sort of copper. That's how he knew 'bout us. Said we had been specially chosen and offered us good money for two months' work."

"Inspector Ridgeley?"

"Aye, that's him."

Holmes exchanged another glance with Mendoza who merely smiled at the disclosure. My colleague then jumped up excitedly and directed a question at him: "Are you comfortable to travel with Mr Jamieson to retrieve your dog?" Mendoza grinned from ear to ear and then looked very directly at Jamieson. "More than content, Mr Holmes, more than content…"

"Good. And should there be any problems, you must despatch a telegram to me immediately. In the absence of any further communication from you, I would ask that you meet Dr Watson and I, here, at Baker Street, at nine o'clock tomorrow. I am optimistic that we will have further news for you then."

The two men headed off. Holmes watched from the upstairs window as they hailed a cab and departed. I could see the first droplets of rain beginning to tap lightly against the glass. "A fascinating development, Watson, and much to our advantage." He pulled his pocket watch from his waistcoat and glanced at the time. "The main proceedings of the Radicant Munificent Society begin at twelve o'clock sharp. We have sufficient time to send a quick telegram to Inspector Athelney Jones before making our way to the East End. Looks like we will need umbrellas, Macintosh's and.....I might just take something I have been working on in recent weeks..."

He disappeared into the makeshift laboratory at the back of the study, moving glass vials, opening drawers and generally clanking around, before emerging - somewhat jubilantly - with two small metal canisters in his hand.

I was at once intrigued. "New toys, Holmes?"

"Yes, they may prove useful. You'll have to wait to see what they do!"

We headed downstairs and equipped ourselves with raincoats and umbrellas from the cast iron stand within the hallway. Holmes placed the mysterious canisters in an outer pocket of his Macintosh and selected a bowler from one of the coat hooks. We then set off on foot to the nearest telegraph office, the umbrellas protecting us from the worst of the now heavy downfall.

It took Holmes but a few minutes to compose his telegram to Athelney Jones and when we re-emerged from the telegraph office found that the downpour had intensified. The streets had cleared of walkers and every available hansom was suddenly in demand. Sheltering as best we could within the entrance to a large department store, we waited almost twenty minutes before securing a ride to Shadwell.

Sat in the cab, I used the opportunity to quiz Holmes, who had, to that point, been wholly uncommunicative. "Why the need for Athelney Jones?"

He continued to stare ahead, his brow furrowed and his keen eyes alert to every sight and sound as the hansom moved slowly through the busy traffic of the Shadwell Fish Market. "A precaution, Watson, as I have a strong feeling that Merrill-Adams's campaign of intimidation is about to enter a new phase. With Inspector Ridgeley's help he has hired a dozen well-known heavies for a brief, but timely period. I am certain that he has clear plans for them and will use his inaugural public address to the recipients of the society's penny bundles, to try and ferment further attacks on Jewish business owners. I have asked Jones to muster as many plain clothes officers as he can. As well as keeping the peace, I am sure that he will be keenly interested to know what Inspector Ridgeley is up to when not serving as a metropolitan officer."

He gave the side of the carriage a sharp knock and the obliging cabbie pulled over, depositing us outside a shabby baker's shop with a cracked front window and an unappealing display of cottage loaves and assorted pastries. Holmes tipped the driver and nodded his appreciation, before once more opening up his umbrella. He then strode off along a narrow thoroughfare, tip-toeing around puddles of muddy water and side-stepping the itinerant labourers, streetwalkers and beggars that continued with their activities despite the foul weather. A short while later we emerged on to a more expansive open street which appeared to house a great many artisan businesses and tradesmen.

The pungent smell of fish had not diminished as we approached our destination - a large Presbyterian meeting house, outside of which was assembled a crowd of many hundreds; men, women and children, most of whom looked distressingly down-trodden and wretched. We made our way through the teeming masses and ducked into a small public house just beyond the hall. Inspector Jones and his men were not difficult to spot - even out of their uniforms the men looked healthy, well-fed and neatly groomed compared to the majority of the drinkers and revellers around us. There was a considerable hubbub within the tap room and while nodding to a couple of the constables I recognised, noted that Holmes was deep in conversation with the cheery-looking Inspector.

We had planned our arrival to perfection. With no time to contemplate even a half pint of ale, another noise then demanded our attention. Back outside in the street, a brass band had struck up with a stirring rendition of *God Save the Queen*, and moments later we were able to watch as a procession of musicians filed past in the direction of the meeting house accompanied by all manner of jugglers, plate-spinners, gymnasts and dancers. Tucked in behind them was a lone figure in a dark blue hooded cloak carrying a long gold mace, whom I guessed to be Morley Merrill-Adams. Behind him, and walking two abreast, were the remaining two dozen members of the Radicant Munificent Society. Their cloaks were a variety of individual colours and on the back of each was displayed the crest and motto of the society. Like their leader, all of the men were hooded, protecting them from the rain and neatly preserving their anonymity.

With a quick nod from Inspector Jones, the undercover officers move swiftly towards the door. Holmes and I followed. Out on the street they began to disperse, mingling in with others following the parade, but remaining in view of Athelney Jones at all times. Up ahead, the brass band had come to a halt outside the Presbyterian hall and played out the final few bars of the National Anthem. The crowd then fell silent, with those amassed outside the meeting house parting, to allow the president of the society to approach the double doors. Having raised the ceremonial mace, he struck the right door firmly and, with continuing pageantry, was then admitted to the building by a uniformed doorman. In single file, the remaining members of the society were then granted entry to the hall before the door was once again closed.

The spectacle was greeted by a loud cheer from the crowd and the silence was from that time broken. I peeked at Holmes and raised both eyebrows. He neatly interpreted my query and whispered: "At twelve-fifteen the double doors will be open to the public. Those wishing to receive a penny bundle make their way to the left of the hall where they line up to be received by the president of the society. Of course, the event is strictly choreographed so that only two hundred bundles are given out. I imagine that some of the hired heavies will ensure that order is kept. Many others attend the ceremony in a civic capacity – local worthies and aldermen, who are invited by the society to maintain its charade of respectability."

Holmes had clearly done his research, for the doors of the hall opened, as predicted, at a quarter-past the hour. Two burly roughs stood either side of the door scrutinising those who began to flood into the hall and every so often stepping forward to prevent the admission of one or two of the more inebriated or troublesome characters who presented themselves. A short while later we found ourselves admitted to the spacious interior of the meeting house and when the hall was judged to be full, the large entrance doors were closed behind us.

I followed Holmes as he sidled down the central aisle of the hall aiming to get as close to the front as he could. I caught occasional glimpses of Athelney Jones's men who looked to be doing the same. We seated ourselves in the plain wooden stalls to the left of the central pulpit, removing our raincoats and placing them and the umbrellas at our feet. Stood along the wall to our side, I could see three orderly queues of men, women and children who were eagerly awaiting the handout of the penny bundles.

It was some time before all of the spectators were finally seated and the atmosphere within the high-ceilinged hall was uncomfortably humid given the large number of damp and clammy bodies that had been admitted. On carefully positioned chairs along the front of the hall sat the shrouded members of the Radicant Munificent Society, each with his head bowed. Occupying a central position within the group was the president in his distinctive dark blue cloak, the cuffs, belt and edging of which was adorned with expensive gold braiding.

From somewhere to the rear of the building came the sound of a loud bell, the striking of which prompted all of the society to finally remove their hoods and the hall to descend into silence. We were now looking into the faces of this most secretive association of men. A few looked distinctly uncomfortable, although most seemed unperturbed by the attention. Morley Merrill-Adams was a stout, barrel-chested man of some sixty years. His hair was completely grey, as was the thick moustache that sat beneath his thin, beak-like, nose. And there was more than a touch of arrogance about the man as he stuck out his chin and looked left and right towards his compatriots with a distinctly paternalistic air.

To his right sat an extremely tall man with short dark hair and a pugnacious look. The long scar on his left cheek confirmed that this was Inspector Ridgeley. I wondered if he had already spotted one or two of his fellow metropolitan officers who were all now seated within the first three rows of the meeting house. His general demeanour suggested that he was not concerned about anything going on around him.

The bell sounded a second time, at which Merrill-Adams rose to address his audience. He had a deep Lancastrian accent and the timbre of his voice carried well across the hall. He introduced himself and said a little about the history of the society, focusing – naturally – on the more benevolent aspects of its heritage. He then invited the charitable beneficiaries to come forward, one at a time, to receive their penny bundles before being shepherded towards the back of the hall. The whole event was neatly orchestrated and when the final bundle had been passed into the grasping hand of the last recipient, Merrill-Adams made his way up into the central pulpit for his keynote address. I felt Holmes shuffle beside me, reaching down calmly to reclaim his Macintosh from the floor.

The president was a gifted speaker who knew how to work his audience. And it was clear that he had arranged for some of his henchmen to position themselves around the hall, and - following some pre-arranged cues - to clap and cheer at intervals to encourage the wider support of the crowd. He began with some observations on the poverty of the East End and the descent into crime and drunkenness which afflicted so many. He talked about the struggles of the established church to address the moral degradation of the local population and the way that compulsory education was failing to instil within the young the habits of industry. And he blamed politicians for doing little to sort out the source of the problems.

All of this was widely applauded. But then he came to specify what he believed to be the root cause of all the concerns he had alluded to. His discourse took on a darker character and began to prompt some disquiet within the hall. His brazen and explicit attack on the Jewish community led some of those present to stand up and leave the hall in disgust. As they did so, others jeered and heckled them.

I cannot find it within myself to set down even a flavour of the words and vitriol to which we were subjected in those moments, as more and more of the crowd were whipped up and began to cheer widely at Merrill-Adams's finger-pointing. He was about to suggest some of the ways in which the audience could 'tackle the Jewish threat' when Holmes took it upon himself to bring an end to the tirade.

With a swift movement of his right arm I saw him toss one of the small metal canisters he had brought with him to the left of the hall, and then stooped to roll the other along the floor to my right. There were two small explosions as both canisters were suddenly ignited and began to produce prodigious volumes of thick grey smoke. A state of pandemonium broke out across the hall, instantly drowning out Merrill-Adams's words, with people jumping up from their seats and jostling to move to the rear of the building.

Holmes watched with evident glee and glanced across to Athelney Jones, who returned a nervous smile, before rising and nodding to three or four of his senior officers. Some moved towards the front of the hall in order to prevent members of the Radicant Munificent Society from escaping, while others began to tackle the agitated and bewildered henchmen.

The smoke lingering across the front section of the hall was now so dense that it was difficult to see anything at all to a height of about five feet. Holmes grabbed my arm and pointed in the direction of the central pulpit which was just visible above the smog. Merrill-Adams was nowhere to be seen.

Spluttering in the acrid fumes we edged forward. To our right, two broad-shouldered constables were placing handcuffs on a stunned-looking Inspector Ridgely. Athelney-

Jones looked to be rounding up other cloaked members of the society.

As we reached the central pulpit, Holmes shouted and gesticulated once again – this time in the direction of a small door on the far wall beyond the podium. We wasted no time in making for the exit to find that it opened on to a series of small ancillary rooms. The first was a long cloakroom with a small water closet to the right. Holmes pressed on while I paused briefly to check that it was empty. When I re-emerged, I saw him pass into a further room beyond. As I attempted to do the same, I was brought to an abrupt halt. Holmes stood motionless, a little to the right of the doorway. To his side was Morley Merrill-Adams, who now held a small handgun to my colleague's temple. I froze, instantly castigating myself for not having my own firearm to hand.

Merrill-Adams had a haunted look. The colour had drained from his face and his eyes were wild with fear; gone was the assured composure we had witnessed only moments before. He cast a quick glance in my direction before refocusing on Holmes. It was the latter who spoke first. "And what do you plan to do now, Mr Merrill-Adams? There is no exit from the building at this end of the hall, or you would have departed before we arrived."

The banker gritted his teeth. "It appears that you have the advantage, gentlemen. You seem to know who I am, but I have no idea who you are."

"My name is Sherlock Holmes. The colleague to my rear is Dr John Watson."

"I see. Then I am indeed in esteemed company. And were the other men with you? They seem to have done a very good job of disrupting the legitimate meeting of a charitable organisation."

Despite the obvious threat facing him, Holmes snorted with derision. "There is nothing charitable about your robberies and intimidation. The other men are officers from Scotland Yard. They have just arrested Inspector Ridgeley, the corrupt officer you thought would protect you from official scrutiny. They know all about your legitimate role as the head of Pendleton-Lyons, but are just a little more interested in your felonious activities."

We could still hear the considerable clamour coming from the main hall. Merrill-Adams continued to hold the gun to Holmes's head for some seconds and then allowed his arm to drop slowly, before casting the weapon on to the floor. With a final attempt at defiance he merely added: "Then I wait to see the proof you have to support these very serious assertions."

\*\*\*\*\*\*\*\*\*\*\*\*\*\*\*\*\*\*\*\*\*\*\*\*

It was shortly before nine o'clock the following morning that Holmes and I finally had a chance to catch up on the previous day's events. Following the arrest of Merrill-Adams, we had spent some time giving our statements to Inspector Jones at Scotland Yard. Holmes had then offered to stay on and provide him with further information about the nefarious activities of the Radicant Munificent Society. I had left at that point to return home to my wife, promising to call in at Baker Street early the next day.

Holmes was in the very best of moods when I arrived; updating his private files with some of the information he had gleaned on the case. In contrast to the day before, the Capital was bathed in warm summer sunlight and temperatures were predicted to climb steadily throughout the coming hours. I refused the offer of a coffee and cigar and sat down to quiz him on a few outstanding aspects of the case.

"What were those canisters you used yesterday? I've never seen smoke bombs quite like those!"

He grinned mischievously. "No, Watson. Something I have developed following our little success a few months back – in the case you entitled *A Scandal in Bohemia*. You may remember the small plumber's smoke rocket we used to good effect. I thought it might be useful to produce a more potent device of my own. My smoke bombs used potassium chlorate as an oxidising agent and refined sugar as a fuel. To these I added some sodium bicarbonate to dampen the heat and a powdered organic dye, which first evaporates and then condenses into tiny particles, to produce the impressive smoke effect. The use of the metallic casing enabled me to include a robust ignition system to create the initial spark."

"Quite remarkable, I'd say - although Athelney Jones didn't seem too impressed."

"No," he chuckled, "I think he suspects I may have terrorist leanings!"

"And his thoughts on the evidence against Merrill-Adams?"

"Jones is almost certain that the robberies and campaign of intimidation are the work of Merrill-Adams and Ridgeley only. The others seem to know nothing about what has gone on and a number have suggested that this may signal an inglorious end to the clandestine organisation. Jones also has little doubt that charges can be brought against both men to secure their conviction and ensure long prison sentences."

"Then a successful conclusion all round."

"I would say so, Watson. Let us hope that Mr Mendoza concurs."

The familiar ring of the doorbell announced the arrival of the man himself. Mendoza fairly sprinted up the stairs to join us in the consulting room. He seemed flushed with excitement as he shook our hands with some vigour.

"So, the dog is safe then, Mr Mendoza?" said Holmes.

"Yes, indeed, Mr Holmes, but there has been some considerable talk down at the synagogue that members of the Radicant Munificent Society were arrested yesterday following an attempt to burn down the Presbyterian meeting house. Can that be true?"

I struggled to suppress a laugh at the thought that Holmes had now been cast in the role of an arsonist. My colleague maintained his composure with admirable aplomb. Over the course of the next fifteen to twenty minutes he took Mendoza through the full details of what had actually occurred and confirmed that Merrill-Adams and Ridgeley were likely to face lengthy prison sentences if convicted. He then indicated that Inspector Jones was keen to speak to Mendoza as part of the investigation and might require him to give evidence at the eventual trial. Mendoza was delighted to hear the news.

"Then you have brought this case to the most satisfactory of conclusions for a great many people, gentlemen. You have my most profound thanks. Now, I trust you will forgive the presumption on my part - for I do not think we discussed fees at any stage, Mr Holmes – but I have taken the liberty of choosing these small gifts for you both, which I hope will serve as some recompense for the considerable dangers you faced on this endeavour."

He pulled from an outside pocket and handed to us two small, black, wooden boxes, exquisitely decorated with inlaid gold leaf and bearing our full names in block capitals. At his beckoning, we opened the boxes to find inside a set of gold and diamond-encrusted cufflinks, complete with matching tiepins. The craftsmanship was exceptional and I could but wonder at the value of such a set. He then handed Holmes a long white envelope, containing a cheque, indicating that it should, "...more than cover your anticipated fees and any incidental expenses you have incurred in the course of your investigations."

Holmes took the envelope with a polite thank you and proceeded to open it. Notwithstanding his intrinsic ability to present a deadpan expression in any moment of heightened tension or acute emotion, my colleague could not in this case disguise his astonishment. His jaw dropped, and he merely passed the cheque across to me as if seeking confirmation that the amount written on it was indeed real. It was written out for the sum of *five thousand pounds*.

Our client left us not long after. Holmes sat quietly for a few moments after his departure and then sprang up with unexpected gusto. "Come, Watson, time and tide wait for no man! I neglected to tell you, but I have a new case involving a steam engine, a human sacrifice and a disputed family legacy. It may prove to be one of the most remarkable adventures we have ever embarked upon!"

It was a measure of his highly-ordered mind and general self-composure that every thought, feeling and action had to be rationalised within his universal psyche. He cared not for surprises and Mendoza's unexpected generosity had triggered within him a disquieting sensation beyond his comprehension. I knew instantly that his call to action was merely an attempt to dislodge such a debilitating emotion.

It was less than a week later, while I was attending to an elderly patient, that I received an unexpected letter amongst the surgery's post. There was no mistaking the hand, and it was with some curiosity that I opened the envelope, eager to know why Holmes was writing to me when he had had ample opportunity to communicate with me face to face in the days before. To my astonishment, the envelope contained a banker's draft, made out for *two thousand, five hundred pounds*. A small handwritten note accompanied the cheque. On it were just three words: "Spend it wisely!"

**Note:** Daniel Abraham Aaron Mendoza (1764-1836) was a genuine prize-fighter and pugilist who became the sixteenth heavyweight boxing champion of England. While he had a great many children and grandchildren, the character of Samuel Mendoza is a product of the author's imagination and any resemblance to an actual person, living or dead, is entirely coincidental.

# 5. The Strange Missive of Germaine Wilkes

*London – Monday, 25th May 1891 – It will come as no surprise to many of you who have long followed the exploits of my dear friend and colleague, Sherlock Holmes, to learn that one of the most frequently asked questions I am now faced with is, "When did you first learn of Professor James Moriarty?" It is a query to which I have given much thought and some speculation in recent days, imagining that the name had first come to my attention only a month or so ago. But yesterday, while looking back over a sheaf of notes I had retained from the late summer of 1887, I was finally able to pinpoint with some uneasiness the moment when Holmes first alerted me to the existence of his arch-nemesis.*

I had called in at Baker Street just before ten o'clock on a bright and sunny Saturday morning in August to find Holmes in an ebullient mood. Apart from looking somewhat tired and pallid, he appeared to be in reasonable health and was quick to jump up from his favourite armchair to greet me as I entered the upstairs room at Mrs Hudson's direction.

"Watson, my dear fellow! What a pleasant surprise, and such perfect timing. I am currently awaiting the arrival of Inspector MacDonald, whose earlier telegram informs me that he has a conundrum that Scotland Yard cannot solve. I trust that will serve as a sufficient inducement to get you to linger a while and share a fresh pot of tea with me. I am sure that your wife will not begrudge you a couple of hours in my company – especially now that you have purchased the birthday present she has wanted for some time."

"Indeed Holmes, that sounds splendid," I replied, "but I am at a loss to know how you could possibly have ascertained the nature of my earlier errand."

I could see the glint in his eye as he realised that I was, as ever, confounded by his powers of deduction. "A simple case of pulling together the discernible clues into a workable hypothesis. A couple of months ago you mentioned to me that your wife was keen to fill your newly-decorated parlour with a suitable piece of furniture. You joked about how much that was likely to cost and how much time you had already spent trying to find an ornate chair or couch that would suffice. When we were last together – less than two weeks ago – walking back to 221B, we passed Druce's Furniture Showroom on the corner of Baker Street. I noted that your eyes dwelt a little too long on the stylish chaise longue that Mr Druce has positioned very cannily in his window display. And armed with the knowledge that your wife's birthday falls in early September, I had thought at the time that you were minded to buy the piece and had hesitated only because of the hefty price tag."

"You are not wrong there," I admitted, disappointed that my thoughts and thriftiness had been so transparent. "But how did you know that I went back today to purchase the couch?"

"A few tell-tale observations to add to what I already knew," he continued. "As you always do, you carry your cheque book in its leather case in your inside top pocket. The case is slightly too big for the pocket and has a habit of poking out occasionally. Realising that this is a Saturday, and your bank is therefore closed, I can only speculate that the cheque book has been used to make a significant purchase. And reflecting on the fact that Druce's Showroom lies less than two-hundred-and-twenty yards from here, it seems reasonable to assume that you have already purchased the chaise longue and thought you would call in to see me while you were so close to your old haunt. Furthermore, your obvious smile and upbeat humour this morning suggests that the transaction has not been too damaging, by which I mean that you successful haggled with dear old Druce to give you a discount on the item in question."

I could not hide my astonishment, but was happy to point out a minor blemish in his otherwise comprehensive account. "Holmes, you clearly do not know Druce well at all. A discount was out of the question. What I successfully negotiated was free delivery of the piece on my wife's birthday!"

We both laughed as Holmes poured the tea and then raised an eyebrow at a further knock on the front door, before exclaiming: "Excellent, MacDonald is as punctual as ever."

Having poured another cup and exchanged some pleasantries with the man from Scotland Yard, Holmes was keen to get on with the business at hand. The amiable detective was happy to oblige.

"Aye, it's a puzzle alright. For some time, we've been aware that a gang of bank thieves has been planning some raids in the city. They are led by a one-time banknote forger called Germaine Wilkes, an American by birth. Late last night, one of my men spotted Wilkes walking through Westminster and promptly arrested him. We now have him under lock and key at the Yard, but he is proving to be most uncooperative and saying very little. At some point we will have to release him."

I was the first to interject. "Surely, you have sufficient evidence to hold him. Was he carrying anything that could incriminate him or provide a link to his known accomplices?"

MacDonald looked crestfallen and explained that he had spent all night interrogating Wilkes without success. He then reached inside his tweed frockcoat and drew out a folded sheet of paper. "The only piece of information we managed to find on him was this," he added, handing the opened note to my colleague. "The difficulty we have Mr Holmes, is that we can't make head nor tail of it. And knowing that you're a man who's accomplished at solving all manner of riddles, we thought it might be one for you."

Holmes had fallen silent as he gazed intently at the page before him. His eyes rapidly scanned the missive and then he broke off, looked across at me and held out the note. "What do you make of it, Watson?"

I held in my hands a single sheet of foolscap paper, on which was printed the following:

*Right 2, Left 3, 1, Right 3, 3, Left 2 – NO HIDE BIRDIE ID*

Eager to make some sense of the seemingly unintelligible message before me, I thought of Holmes's methods and began to apply the same degree of scrutiny. "It seems to me that we have two parts to this message," I ventured. "The first few words suggest an instruction of some kind; perhaps a marching step, a map direction or even the coding sequence required to open up a safe or bank vault. The second part, in capital letters, may well be the substance of the communiqué, the real point that the author wishes to convey."

Holmes was unusually enthusiastic in his response. "Bravo, Watson! I concur with you completely. The message does indeed appear to have two distinct parts and it would seem logical that the first is some form of instruction or direction-marker for the reader. What else?"

Egged on, I then suggested that the form of the note seemed significant. "Why bother to have this typeset and printed when it could so easily have been handwritten?"

This time is was MacDonald who replied with some eagerness. "My thoughts exactly, Dr Watson. And if you look at the back of the note you will see that the imprint of the type has gone through the page, which tells us that the message was hand-typed rather than printed."

"Indeed it was," concurred Holmes. "A fact that we can take to be highly significant, I suspect. So, do you know who sent the note, MacDonald?"

The Inspector looked bemused. "No, how could I possibly know? Wilkes has refused to say anything about the note and where it came from."

"My dear Inspector. I thought your intelligence on Wilkes and his cohort of bank thieves might have extended as far as the knowledge that, while they are believed to be operating as a discrete gang, they have much broader connections to a large criminal network operating across London, parts of Europe, and as far as North America. It should come as no surprise that Wilkes hails from the other side of the pond. My contacts tell me that he was chosen specifically for his role by the real puppet-master in the criminal fraternity."

MacDonald tried to hide his frustration, but realised that Holmes had the upper hand. "So, Mr Holmes, who do *you* believe sent the note to Wilkes?"

Holmes looked at him directly, and addressed him without a hint of conceit: "I have no doubt whatsoever, that this message was sent by the very person who directs all of the major operations of the criminal network I have described. That person is none other than Professor James Moriarty. I have it on good authority that Wilkes had previously been Moriarty's favoured lieutenant in a counterfeiting ring that once operated out of Cincinnati."

"How can you be so sure, Holmes? And who is this Professor – I've never heard you mention him before?"

Holmes turned his gaze towards me, and for a split second a look of fear passed across his face. "That is because I had hoped to spare you, indeed protect you, from the knowledge that we now have a criminal mastermind operating with relative impunity from a base in London – a man who is more than a match for any of the crime agencies which exist in New York, Paris or London itself. He is cunning and formidable and exceedingly dangerous. By day, he masquerades as an academic, eminent in his field, mentoring the very brightest student minds. By night, he casts off the gown – operating under a different cloak – and directing the endeavours of a very different class of followers. Make no mistake, Watson, Moriarty is behind this, and the less you know of him, the better it will be for your sake and your wife's."

The casual reference to my beloved wife had the desired effect and I offered no further challenge. I could see also that MacDonald had been listening intently, taking in this new information and looking slightly awestruck at Holmes's assertions. In the silence that followed, it was he who spoke first.

"So, where does all that leave us with this note, Mr Holmes? Are you able to tell me what it means and whether I should continue to hold Wilkes?"

"I am sure I can crack the meaning behind this communication and set you on the right path. But I will need some time and your indulgence for a short while yet, as I need to make a brief excursion into town. It is now half-past ten.

Could I suggest that we reconvene back here in Baker Street in two hours' time? I will instruct Mrs Hudson to have waiting for us a light luncheon of bread and cold ham."

MacDonald was visibly relieved. "That sounds wonderful! I am very grateful to you, Mr Holmes, and will take my leave. I will be back promptly at 12.30, as you suggest."

When MacDonald had gone, I took the opportunity to try and get Holmes to talk more about the enigmatic Professor Moriarty, but all of my gentle questioning brought little by way of a response. "I can tell you nothing further at this stage, Watson. I really do have to go into town. A short spell of shopping should do the trick. I should then be in a position to tell you the substance of the message from Moriarty."

Without further explanation he was off, heading down the stairs of 221B, through the front door, and out into the street before I could even think to ask if he wanted me to join him. I resolved to await his return and find out whether he really could make sense of the strange note to Germaine Wilkes.

In Holmes's absence, I read the headline features in *The Times*, keen to find out if there was anything in the press that might shed some light on Wilkes's activities or the shadowy network of crooks that were being directed by Moriarty. The big news of the day was that a major financial fraud had been uncovered in a provincial bank in the south of England. There was also news that a cruise ship had run aground off the coast of Cornwall, with the loss of ten lives. Equally disturbing was the announcement that the previous evening a British politician had been found dead, close to Westminster Bridge. The report said that Augustus Waldringfield, the Member of Parliament for Chippenham East, had been found stabbed to death. It speculated that his death may have been linked to his much publicised opposition to the Irish Home Rule bill which had been defeated in the Lords the previous year. The article went on to say that it was well known that Waldringfield had been a fierce critic of the Fenian Brotherhood, the group thought most likely to have carried out the attack.

A little over an hour after he had departed, Holmes was back in Baker Street, clutching a large box which I imagined was the result of his mysterious shopping expedition. I was quick to express my surprise at his behaviour.

"Holmes, in all the time that I have known you, I cannot recollect another occasion on which you have left an active case in order to spend time purchasing something for yourself. Please tell me that this is some curious aberration on your part!"

"Watson, your instincts have not deserted you. This was no routine purchase, my friend."

He began to unpack the box, revealing a black mechanical instrument, along the front of which were positioned numerous keys, marked by different letters of the alphabet and other recognisable symbols. With care, he set the instrument down on his writing desk, and stepped back to admire its appearance.

"I have here a marvel of the modern age. A Sholes and Glidden patent typewriting machine, manufactured by the American firm of E. Remington and Sons. It was first produced in 1875, and is becoming more popular on both sides of the Atlantic, replacing the need for costly typesetting, and enabling even the most humble of offices to produce their own printed stationery. The arrangement of the keys enables the typist to adopt a standard finger position in order to use the machine. With experience, practice and dexterity, I am told that a regular operative can type out at least forty words a minute."

He had heartfelt enthusiasm for this mechanical contraption and proceeded to insert into it a single sheet of paper taken from the drawer of the desk. I felt I had to express my obvious confusion. "I'm sorry Holmes, but I don't see what this has got to do with the note we are trying to decipher?"

"Well, let us return to that very note, before MacDonald reappears. We shall look at it afresh." He spread the note out before us to the right of the typewriter. "Let us consider first its form. The page has been typewritten and deliberately so. Moriarty is telling Wilkes something by the mere fact that he has typed the missive. I believe that the "right, left, right, left" reference and the associated numbers are instructions related to the use of a standard typewriter. To that we will return in a moment."

He now pointed specifically to the second part of the message and read out "NO HIDE BIRDIE ID." "I believe there is a clear message here. Moriarty is saying: 'We can now expose the person who has to date been undercover, unrecognised or otherwise hidden from the public gaze.' 'BIRDIE' is his code for the mole, spy or agent he is referring to."

"But what about this word 'ID', Holmes, what does that suggest?"

"The term 'ID' has a certain American ring to it – a slang term for *identification*. It is not one which our British policing colleagues have yet adopted with any great enthusiasm, but the Police Department of New York has been pioneering in its work to provide IDs for all of the major felons it wishes to apprehend. Inspector Thomas Byrnes's *Professional Criminals of America* was published in September last year and provides both written descriptions and photographs of the offenders concerned. I only know this because I was asked by the capable Inspector to contribute intelligence to some of the descriptions used in the book. For the purposes of our note, Moriarty is saying to Wilkes that the target's identity can now be revealed."

I was still confused. "So, who is the subject of the note? How could Moriarty be sure that Wilkes would know exactly who to target without risking detection if the note was intercepted?"

"A good point, Moriarty needed to be specific. But this is a clever piece of subterfuge. Alongside the main communication, there is a second, hidden message, which precisely answers your question. Let us now turn to that."

He pointed his long index finger at the main body of the text. "I thought at first that the hidden message was a simple process of letter substitution, with each different character of the 'NO HIDE BIRDIE ID' line representing an alternative letter in a traditional cypher. I was quick to discard the thought though, as there were no obvious solutions and it would have been unlikely that, as a mathematical genius, Moriarty would have relied on such an obviously easy code."

"Would the message be an anagram in that case?" I interjected, realising instantly that a straightforward anagram was also unlikely. "After all, the number sequence '2, 3, 1, 3, 3, 2', contained within what we believe to be the instructions, do add up to fourteen, the number of letters in the main message."

"That is true, but try as I might, Watson, I could think of no sensible anagram from the letters in the sentence. I did, however, come up with one line that I thought you might like as a medical man – 'I'd bid heroin die.'" I ignored the jibe, resisting the temptation to castigate him as I had so often for his casual drug use. Holmes returned to the subject of the typewriter.

"I am convinced that the keyboard will provide the solution to this puzzle," he said, placing his hands in the correct position for typing. "The sales assistant was most insistent that the fingers be positioned accordingly. Now, following the instructions in the note, we move our finger position one key to the 'right' and type the first two letters out as if we were routinely typing the word 'NO'. His fingers struck the keys accordingly and the letters "MP" appeared on the paper. He then tapped a long key at the bottom of the keyboard which he informed me was the "spacebar".

"Now we are instructed to move to the 'left.'" He repositioned his fingers to the left of the standard typing position and typed what would have been "HIDE", being careful to use the spacebar to separate the letters into two words – one of three letters, the second of just one. On the paper, the newly-typed words read "GUS W." At this point I remained unconvinced that Holmes" experiment would bear any useful fruit.

Following the same logic and procedure, Holmes finished typing out the short sentence. Having done so, he pulled the newly-typed page from the typewriter and retrieved an ink pen from the desk drawer, adding a few words atop the typed sentence.

"Let us see what we now have, Watson! Put together, the two sentences read: 'No hide birdie ID – MP Gus W not for us.'"

Recollecting the earlier article in *The Times*, the message now made perfect sense to me. "The dead politician, Holmes! The MP for Chippenham East, Augustus Waldringfield – he was found murdered last night!"

"So it would appear, dear fellow. And his demise was at the hands of Wilkes and not the Fenian Brotherhood. That invention was most likely promulgated by Moriarty himself to throw the suspicion off his criminal associates. What you might not yet have read, Watson, is that Waldringfield has also now been linked to the major fraud case involving the Surrey Shires Bank, of which he was one of the directors. I think we can take it that Moriarty or one of his associates had found out about the bank's fraudulent activities, and had then tried to blackmail the MP with the information, threatening to reveal both the crime and the politician's link to it, if he did not bend to Moriarty's will. The outcome of the matter suggests that Waldringfield had refused to yield to the Professor's demands, and Wilkes was therefore instructed by this note to go public with the information about the MP's nefarious activities. Whether or not Moriarty had gone as far as to sanction murder, we may never know."

At that point, a heavy footfall on the stairs alerted us to the return of Inspector MacDonald. When he entered the room, the detective looked tired and dejected. "I have bad news, I'm afraid. It seems that sometime this morning, after I had left him to come here, Wilkes received a visit at Scotland Yard from someone purporting to be his legal representative. Having spent just a few moments with Wilkes, the man asked to be released from the holding cell and left the building. The supervising officer said that Wilkes had appeared to be fine at that point and had expressed some confidence that he would soon be released from custody. However, when the same officer returned to check on the prisoner some twenty minutes later, he found the banknote forger in the last throes of death. It seems his visitor had dispensed some form of poison, and Wilkes died shortly afterwards. I guess that puts an end to our speculation about the puzzling note, Mr Holmes."

It was Holmes's turn to look dejected. "That is troubling news, MacDonald, and I can only apologise for having underestimated the extraordinary lengths that Moriarty would go to in covering his role in this sad state of affairs. Dr Watson will no doubt convey to you over lunch the full details of what we have uncovered, having deciphered the note, and our speculation as to its links to some of the recent stories which have appeared in the press. For my part, I will leave you in his excellent company. I find myself suddenly without an appetite and in need of some fresh London air."

With no further explanation, Holmes left us to the fine spread which Mrs Hudson had prepared, and we spent the next hour discussing the meaning of the note and the ramifications of the case.

In the two weeks that followed, I saw very little of my colleague, immersed as I was in the celebrations for my wife's birthday. That, at least, had been a great success – the chaise longue being considered a most perfect centrepiece for our new yellow parlour.

When I did eventually feel comfortable to bring up the subject of the Wilkes note, Holmes was demonstrably reticent to discuss the matter in any further detail. With a dismissive shake of the head, he requested only that I promise him two things – firstly, never to make public the strange case of the typewritten missive, and secondly, to never let him forget that Moriarty might one day be the cause of his undoing. It is with more than a tinge of sadness that I convey to you, dear reader, as I sit here reflecting on the terrible events that have occurred at the Reichenbach Falls, I fear I have let Holmes down on both counts.

# 6. A Case of Poetic Injustice

"We've seen this before, Watson..." My colleague held before him a single sheet of paper on which I could see some closely typed script. "...the distinctive stationery, the consistent use of the Merritt typewriter and the familiar hint of hair oil - it seems that Edwin Halvergate is once again writing poetry and has seen fit to enclose one of his compositions in this letter to me, which was hand-delivered only a short while ago."

Facing a roaring log fire, I had, to that point, been engrossed in one of my monthly medical journals reading a particularly fascinating news feature. A month before, a dear friend, Dr John Hall-Edwards, had used electromagnetic radiation – or *x-rays* – to create a radiographic image of a surgical needle which had been hidden under the palm of one of his medical colleagues. I could already see the huge potential for using x-rays in a wide range of surgical situations and applauded his pioneering efforts. It was therefore with some reluctance that I placed the journal to one side and looked across at Holmes: "Is that the Halvergate fellow I wrote about recently in *A Study in Verse?*"

"Yes, and it seems that he is, once again, trying to engage my attention. The letter is short on detail but clear enough in its intention."

"Which is?"

Holmes smiled somewhat enigmatically. "To alert me to a particular crime and to point me in the direction of the guilty party."

"I see. And what does this letter say?"

Holmes passed the sheet across to me. It read:

*Mr Sherlock Holmes*
*221B Baker Street*
*Marylebone*
*London*
*9th February 1896*

*My dearest Mr Holmes,*

*You know that I was, initially, not one to expect thanks on your own undertaking. But, in reality, it's been murder. Nevertheless, another haiku verse to guide your endeavours:*

*Note found on dead girl.*
*Reads – Seven, Seven, One, Nine.*
*Clue upturned – a sign?*

*Perhaps she was wearing a short, close-fitting children's jacket, trimmed with fur, or even an eighteenth century wig? You'll have to work it out.*

*Beyond that, be sure to visit a little farmhouse in England, possibly in the Midlands around Netherton.*

*Yours very sincerely,*

*A concerned citizen*


I looked towards my colleague with evident befuddlement. "I wouldn't say the letter was clear at all. He is evidently upset that you failed to acknowledge his role in helping us to clear up that recent business in Birmingham, but the rest of the letter is complete gibberish!"

Holmes chortled. "That's the spirit, Watson! There is something about Halvergate's literary proclivities that also begins to rankle with me. I am all for riddles and conundrums, but sometimes I prefer a man who speaks plainly. His meaning is clear, but I fail to understand why he hides behind this thin veneer of intellectualism. He may once have been a close and astute disciple of Professor Moriarty, but he is certainly no genius."

"So what does the letter mean?"

"Well, you are probably correct to suggest that Halvergate expected me to be more grateful for his earlier assistance, but the first line of the letter is actually coded. The word 'initially' suggests that we should look at the first letter of the words that follow. So, the initial letters of 'not one to expect thanks on your own undertaking' gives us *note to you* – his way of saying that he has some relevant information to impart. The 'in reality' reference then tells us that he has dispensed with the code and is dealing directly with the subject of his communiqué – namely 'murder'."

"And I suppose this haiku verse provides the solution to the crime?"

"Yes. The girl's death is the result of a murder and the poem tells us the name of the killer. The clue is in the note. When inverted or 'upturned', the number 7719 can be read as *bill*."

"I see. But what about the last paragraph and the reference to this 'wig' and 'jacket'. Is he telling us what the victim was wearing?"

Holmes beamed once more. "No, another name for a jacket of that type and an eighteenth century wig is *Spencer*. Taken together, the clues tell us that the murderer is a *Bill*

*Spencer.* Now, let us see whether we can find reference to such a man in my trusty files." He took a couple of steps towards his unique indexing system, retrieved a file and began to flick through: "...Sandell, Scarman, Shelley, Spatchcock...Yes! Here we are...William 'Bill' Spencer...small time heavy, card sharp and fraudster...one five-year stretch in Newgate for grand larceny...known associate of George Cotton, the Turnmill Street forger."

"George Cotton? Now, that name rings a bell."

"Yes, indeed. You will remember him from the enigmatic case of the sightless seer, Francisco Faccini. Cotton was originally a theatrical set designer, with impeccable artistic credentials, who turned to crime and helped many in the London underworld to perpetrate the most audacious of confidence trickeries, deceptions and frauds. In the aftermath of the Faccini case, Cotton was obliged to leave London on pain of death. Within the criminal fraternity, it was widely believed that he had betrayed Faccini and alerted Scotland Yard to the blind man's duplicitous behaviour in extorting large sums of money from wealthy clients with his fake spiritualism and other swindles. When Faccini died of a heart attack during his Old Bailey trial, his Italian family vowed to avenge the death by tracking down and eliminating Cotton and his two accomplices."

"And did they succeed?"

"In the case of Cotton, yes. A year ago he was fatally stabbed with a stiletto knife in a back street on the outskirts of Lille. Carefully positioned on his chest beside the knife, the gendarmerie found a small *King of Hearts* – the calling card of the Faccini family. I am not aware that there have been any other deaths of a similar nature."

"Then it would not be far-fetched to imagine that Bill Spencer was one of the two accomplices still being pursued by the Faccini family."

"Possibly, Watson, but it is too early to speculate. We must have more data before we can begin to draw any conclusions. Our first priority is to ascertain whether the murder referred to in the poem actually occurred." He paused momentarily, placed the file he had been holding on the arm of a chair and moved swiftly towards the window. "Ah ha! Our deliberations are about to be interrupted by the arrival of Inspector Hopkins. I wonder if this will have any bearing on our quest."

Stanley Hopkins looked chilled to the bone when he entered the study. He was carrying his familiar brown derby in one hand and wore a long Ulster jacket. He seemed pleased to see me with Holmes, and I explained briefly that I was back in my old haunt for two nights as my wife was visiting an aged aunt in Edinburgh. It was a good six or seven months since I had last seen the Inspector and I noticed that he had begun to lose his youthful countenance - the distinct bags under his eyes and receding hairline suggesting that his chosen profession was indeed taking its toll.

"Inspector Hopkins, a rare pleasure!" bellowed Holmes, directing our guest towards one of the chairs closest to the fire. "Now, you will have to forgive the presumption, but have you travelled here to announce that a dead body has been found and the only clue to what is undoubtedly murder, is a handwritten note, placed on the deceased's chest and bearing the numbers '7719'?"

Hopkins looked at Holmes quizzically. "I have come about a murder, sure enough, Mr Holmes. A body that was found last night close to Covent Garden...but it wasn't a note placed on his chest, it was a playing card."

"A *King of Hearts* by any chance?" I could not help but interject to the further astonishment of our guest, who merely nodded in confirmation.

It took us a few minutes to convince Hopkins that Holmes and I did not possess any innate ability to conjure up clairvoyant visions. When Holmes had explained how our enquiries were based on a more rational conjecture, Hopkins chuckled: "Well, I am always impressed by your talents, Mr Holmes. At times, it does seem as if you have an incredible aptitude for seeing things that the rest of us do not. But it was Dr Watson's pronouncement that really caught me off-guard!"

Accepting my colleague's offer of a small sherry, Hopkins sat warming himself by the fire while he studied the letter from Edwin Halvergate. "Gentlemen, while I have heard one or two of my colleagues talk about the man, Halvergate seems to be something of an enigma. To my knowledge, he has never faced arrest and has only been pulled in for questioning on a couple of occasions – each time accompanied by his solicitor. If he is the criminal gang master you suggest, he does a good job of shielding himself from the law."

Holmes showed little reaction but fired a question at the Inspector. "What can you tell us about the body that was found last night?"

"Like this Cotton character you mentioned, the man had been stabbed with a stiletto blade. His body was found in a side alley, tucked away behind some discarded vegetable boxes. The doctor who examined the corpse said that the man could not have been dead long before the body was discovered. One of my constables was called to the scene at around nine-thirty. The thick fog that evening had clearly helped the killer - so far, we have found no one who witnessed the crime or saw anybody carrying such a knife."

"And you have no clue as to the identity of the victim?"

"Not yet. He had nothing on him at all. His pockets were completely empty. The only distinguishing marks on his body were a large scar above his left eye and a wasp tattoo on his right forearm."

I saw my colleague's face light up. "Then we are beginning to get somewhere. The wasp tattoo is the symbol under which Halvergate's men operate. I believe that Watson and I will be able to make some headway on this case, but will need a little time. Could I suggest that you visit us again tomorrow, Inspector - around about the same time?"

Hopkins looked delighted and knocked back what remained of his sherry glass. He then rose and stepped quickly across to where Holmes sat, extending his hand. My colleague could barely conceal his wry grin, but accepted the handshake in good faith. "My dear Inspector, I am only too pleased to assist. I do find February to be the dullest of months, so a decent case will help me to shake off this winter chill. I am sure that I will have positive news for you on the morrow..."

************************

I saw little of Holmes in the hour or so beyond Hopkins's visit. The Inspector had hailed a hansom outside Baker Street, but just before he could set off, Holmes had joined him on the pavement, requesting that they share the cab as far as Bow Street. I watched from the upstairs window as the two departed, Holmes having given no explanation for his sudden departure.

When he returned just before lunchtime, I could tell that his short trip had been efficacious and there was no disguising the look of satisfaction on his face. "Watson, you have been contemplating a trip to the theatre this evening. I fear that you will have to postpone the excursion as I am likely to require your services on the Spencer case."

I was about to indicate that I would be delighted to lend my support, but stopped short: "How did you know I was thinking about the theatre? Have you developed a genuine talent for mind reading?"

He was somewhat dismissive in his response. "There is no great mystery. You are a creature of habit. When I see the fresh fingernail clippings in the ashtray beside you and note that you have - in the short time since my departure – cut your nasal hairs and waxed your moustache with evident aplomb, it is a simple matter to deduce that you have conceived such a trip. When we shared this apartment you always followed the self-same pattern."

I was content to let the matter rest and asked him what progress he had made on the case. "I have set the wheels in motion and engaged the services of Wiggins and the Baker Street Irregulars. They are, at this moment, conducting their own enquiries in the Covent Garden area. If there is any fresh information to be gathered, they will discover it." With nothing further to add, he stepped out onto the landing and shouted for Mrs Hudson. Ten minutes later, we were sat at the table in the apartment enjoying a pot of fresh tea and some thickly-cut beef sandwiches.

It was shortly after three o'clock that afternoon when we received word from the Baker Street Irregulars. In a state of some agitation, Holmes had been pacing before a window of the consulting room in anticipation of Charlie Wiggins's arrival. When the fellow finally approached the door to 221B, Holmes was already there to greet him, quickly ushering his loyal lieutenant up the stairs with little by way of a welcome.

It was a lean, well-dressed and darkly handsome man in his mid-twenties who entered the room and greeted me with a broad smile while removing his cap. "Good afternoon, Doctor. It is a pleasure to see you again after so many years. Mr Holmes said you would be here." I returned a compliment, barely able to believe that this was the same character I had met as a youth and had once described as 'a disreputable little scarecrow'.

Holmes was suddenly alive to the reunion being played out before him: "Ah, yes, Watson! Quite the fellow is our Wiggins. In recent years, he has turned the Baker Street Irregulars into something of a private enquiry agency, tracking down errant husbands and missing children. I still rely upon their invaluable support from time to time, although the agreed rate for their services has naturally increased from what it used to be." He gave Wiggins a wink, slipped what looked like three or four guineas into the man's hand and beckoned for him to take a seat in the chair opposite his own.

"Well, well, my boy – what is the word on the street?"

"Very enlightening, Mr Holmes. As you suggested, we asked around about a tall, dark-haired, Italian lady who may have been seen that night on the streets near Covent Garden. Three men remembered seeing such a woman; they said she was hard to miss. And while she did not strike them as a lady of the night, a costermonger recalled seeing her late on, leaving a local tavern, and arm in arm with a shady-looking character with a scar above his eye. From the small amount of conversation he heard, it was clear that she had a foreign accent and he was heavily drunk."

It was I who spoke at this point, addressing my query towards Holmes. "How did you know to ask about such a woman?"

My colleague shrugged and raised his eyebrows. "It seemed most likely. Inspector Hopkins is nothing if not thorough. But he will have assumed that the stiletto killer was a man. We should not then be surprised that his initial enquiries turned up no suspect. Furthermore, until his visit to Baker Street earlier today, he did not know that the calling card left on the body was a clear sign that the Faccini family had exacted some revenge. If I now tell you that the blind Francisco Faccini had but one child - a daughter by the name of Angelina – and the Sicilian family believed firmly in the age-old axiom 'an eye for an eye', you will begin to see where I was heading. Angelina was an attractive and beguiling young woman who worked as an assistant to her late father. Her presence at each séance and confidence trick was every bit as important as that of the sightless seer. She would interact with his clients beforehand, picking up important personal details and sharing these with him before and during each performance through her carefully coded dialogue. George Cotton exposed their working practices to the police and brought an end to their lucrative ventures."

"I see. But you talked about Angelina Faccini in the past tense. Does that mean you believe she is also now dead?"

"Of course – it is the only explanation which fits the facts as we know them. But we need to confirm my suspicions, and quickly too. What else can you tell us, Wiggins?"

"Well, we figured that the woman was unlikely to live locally and had come to Covent Garden specifically because she knew her victim was likely to be there. And we assumed that she must have needed a place to stay – somewhere real close we thought."

Holmes cut in: "A remarkable leap of faith, but a fair working hypothesis. And how accurate did these suppositions prove to be?"

Wiggins grinned. "Perfectly accurate, Mr Holmes. We were only on our third guest house when the landlady at *The Glendower* confirmed that a tall and very striking Italian woman had booked in only two days before. She had paid for the room in advance for a full week and had asked to be left undisturbed during that time, paying extra for the privilege. The landlady was grateful for the extra income at this time of year and having handed over the key had only seen the woman come and go on a couple of occasions. The room has its own private access at the back of the guest house you see."

"Wiggins, your talents are inestimable! I suggest you take us there immediately. Watson, grab your coat and hat. We're off to Covent Garden!"

************************

*The Glendower* in Catherine Street was a modest guest house occupying three storeys. The private room rented by Angelina Faccini was located at the back of the property through a short passageway between it and the adjacent town house. Wiggins led the way, ascending an iron stairway to the second storey and pointing towards a green door at the end of the balcony we now found ourselves on. Holmes stepped forward, his eyes scanning every facet of the solid oak door. He reached for an inside pocket of his long tweed overcoat and removed a set of lock picks. Within seconds, we were in the outer lobby of the room.

We stepped cautiously into the main space of the apartment which housed a large bed and wardrobe. The only light was coming from a small window on the far wall which I imagined overlooked an internal courtyard of the guesthouse. Further along the same wall I could see a door to a bathroom, open slightly, but otherwise shrouded in darkness.

Wiggins and I stood back as Holmes began to peruse every square inch of the room with his silver magnifying glass to hand. At one point, he looked up with apparent delight, holding before him a few items he had removed from the bottom of the wardrobe. He spoke in a hushed tone. "That is most illuminating, my friends. It is clear now why Bill Spencer made such an effort to track down Angelina Faccini. The man she stabbed last night was Walter Spencer, Bill's brother! There are some papers and other personal effects here which she had clearly removed from the body, probably to frustrate the identification of the corpse."

Wiggins was quick to share a thought. "Bill Spencer obviously didn't know that she'd placed those things in the wardrobe, Mr Holmes. Had he done so, I feel sure he would have taken what belonged to his brother."

Holmes and I nodded and the room again fell silent. A few minutes later my colleague had concluded his examination of the bedroom and took a few steps towards the bathroom, the magnifying glass being trained first towards the handle of the door. "I have no doubt we will find the woman's body inside," was all that he added.

He began to push the door open very slowly with a single finger. It yielded to the pressure but stopped short before his arm could be fully extended. He took a single step in through the gap, glanced around and then looked back towards us, nodding simply to indicate that the scene was as he had predicted.

With a gas lamp lit within the bathroom, Holmes continued his examination and then beckoned for us to join him. Wiggins seemed content to stay in the bedroom, having taken a single peep around the door to see the twisted corpse lying on the white tiled floor. I was invited to examine the body, which lay part-way across the back of the door, the head pointed towards a slim copper bath in the corner of the room.

It was clear that Angelina Faccini had been a staggeringly beautiful woman. Tall and slender, with long auburn hair, green eyes and a warm sallow complexion; she was bewitching, even in death. It was clear that she had been strangled and roughly-handled prior to her demise. There was bruising on her neck, arms and chest and one eye was badly swollen, indicating that she had received at least one blow to the face. In her right hand she was still clutching a stiletto dagger, its blade stained with congealed blood, with further droplets spattered close by on the white tiles and on the sleeve of her blue velvet dress.

Holmes squatted down beside me and asked what I made of the scene. "Spencer looks to have interrogated her with some violence. She has not sustained any knife wounds, so I would suggest that she managed to stab him prior to her own death."

"Agreed. I am not sure whether Spencer had set out to kill the woman, but he clearly knew what she looked like and somehow tracked her to this apartment, hoping to find out the details of how Walter had been murdered. There is a distinct boot print at the foot of the front door, suggesting that he had knocked, and, when the door was opened, had prevented her from slamming it shut. Once inside, they argued within the main room and at some point Miss Faccini made a run for the bathroom to retrieve her one remaining stiletto knife. She was clearly a well-organised assassin."

"So you think Spencer chased her in here, was attacked with the knife and then strangled her?"

"Not quite." Holmes stood up to demonstrate, gesticulating with his hands. "The wounds around her throat show that his thumbs were placed on the back of her neck. She had clearly not been too far from his grasp as she ran in here. He began to throttle her, but was unaware that she had reached out and picked up the stiletto which must have been left on the corner of the copper bath. With his grip tightening, and in the last throes of death, she reached back with her right arm and stabbed at him in the chest. When her body had slumped to the floor, he rolled her over to check that she was dead. There are only small traces of blood here and there. Perhaps he only realised he had been stabbed when he saw the knife in her hand."

I tried to envisage the drama unfolding as Holmes had described, but was then struck with a completely different thought. "What happened to the note? Halvergate referred to a note on the body which read '7719' – where is it?"

"Artistic licence, no doubt. There was no note. It was just a ruse to point us in the direction of Bill Spencer. He clearly wanted the small time crook to be arrested for the murder, without it looking as if he had been instrumental in assisting the enquiry. He assumed my ego would be such that I would wish to take full credit for solving the case, without disclosing his role in the affair."

This time it was Wiggins who spoke, from outside the bathroom door. "But why did Halvergate want to incriminate one of his own men, Mr Holmes?"

I looked up at my colleague, fascinated myself to hear his explanation. He frowned for a brief moment and then responded. "That, my dear Wiggins, is the one crucial question in this whole sorry affair. And for an answer, we have to understand the nature of the criminal underworld in this great city. With Professor Moriarty gone, there is no cohesion or control over the myriad of gangs, mobs and lawless fraternities that operate in the underbelly of our

Capital. Edwin Halvergate has ambitions to establish himself as the head of a criminal cartel which can reassert that authority. At this stage, the last thing he wants is an all-out war with the Italian families who have such a strong foothold in one or two key areas. Were it to be known that the two former accomplices of George Cotton – the man who successfully framed the well-respected Francisco Faccini – had been taken on by Halvergate, such a conflict might be unavoidable."

"So what is our next step, Holmes?" I enquired.

"We must leave Wiggins to report to Inspector Hopkins. The police must be told all that we have discovered. You and I must attempt to find Bill Spencer before anyone else can get to him."

"But how do we do that? He could be anywhere."

"I think not. You see we neglected to consider the last line of the letter from Halvergate, waylaid as we were by the arrival of Hopkins this morning." He pulled the letter from inside his jacket and re-read it. "If we consider the line, *Beyond that, be sure to visit a little farmhouse in England, possibly in the Midlands around Netherton,* we have a clue. The initial letters of each word after 'visit' spell out 'Alfie Pitman', the most notorious card sharp in London and landlord of the *White Lion* in Clapham. I would venture that Bill Spencer is secreted away in a room at the hostelry."

Wiggins left us as planned, agreeing to report back to Holmes later that evening after his meeting with Hopkins. It did not take the two of us long to travel across to Clapham. When we arrived at the public house, Holmes wasted no time in pulling Alfie Pitman to one side for a discreet word. He suggested that the landlord might face prosecution for harbouring a murderer. It was sufficient to produce an immediate response, with Pitman confirming that Bill Spencer was indeed being housed in an upstairs bedroom.

Having quietly ascended the stairs to the bedroom concerned, Holmes tapped lightly on the door and announced in a gruff voice remarkably similar to Pitman's: "Pint of Stout for you, Bill."

The door opened instantly and it was a very shocked Bill Spencer who stood before us. He was tall and well-built, but looked drained - his face ashen and his eyes bloodshot. While bare-chested, his midriff was heavily bandaged and a large patch of red staining was visible on his right side. "Who are you? What do you want?"

Holmes stepped forward and placed a foot against the door. "My name is Sherlock Holmes and this is my colleague, Dr Watson. You may have heard of us?"

I thought for one moment that Spencer was about to pass out. His knees threatened to buckle beneath him, but he steadied himself against the doorframe. Realising that the game was up, he opened the door and nodded for us to enter.

The windowless room was plainly furnished: a bed with a filthy discoloured mattress; a small wooden table on which sat an ornate hurricane lamp; and a rickety-looking chair painted in black.

Holmes got straight to the point. "We know that Angelina Faccini wanted revenge for what she believed George Cotton had done to her father. Having pursued and murdered Cotton in France a year ago, she then set out to track down his two associates – you, and your brother, Walter. Unlike Cotton, you had relied on your contacts in London to shield you. And falling in with Edwin Halvergate, you must have believed that his criminal gang would further protect you from your assassin. But last night you were shocked to find out that Walter had been stabbed and a Faccini calling card had been left on his chest. Not content to sit back and await the same fate, you somehow managed to locate Angelina Faccini. Now, she too lies dead."

Spencer had been staring down at the floor while Holmes spoke. Now he looked up slowly with a surprisingly rueful expression. "I know exactly who you are, gentlemen. And it seems your reputation is well deserved. How you seem to know so much about this affair is beyond me, though I cannot deny the truth of it. But you will have to take me at my word when I say that I did not set out to kill Angelina, even though she had killed my brother."

"Then the two of you were lovers at one time?"

Spencer grimaced. "It's little wonder that Halvergate is obsessed with you, Mr Holmes. Was that a guess, or did you know that Angelina and I had a short-lived romance?"

It was Holmes's turn to frown. "No guesswork, I can assure you, but a reasoned line of enquiry. You see I have been considering how George Cotton managed to know so much about Francisco Faccini's fraudulent activities. His testimony at the Old Bailey was detailed and damning; dates, times, contacts, sums of money. Everything needed to secure the conviction. There must have been someone close to the family providing this information, so it occurred to me that Cotton may have asked you to take on that role. And having done so, you fell for the man's daughter."

"It wasn't planned that way. The feud between Cotton and Faccini went right back to the early days when they both competed on the same turf, conning punters out of their money with fake spirits and bogus predictions. Faccini took exception to Cotton, seeing him as a young pretender, with his elaborately-crafted stage sets and lighting. Cotton was constantly looking for an opportunity to shut down the old man's operation and suggested that I get close to him to find a way of doing it.

"I heard that Faccini needed some muscle for the few occasions when his stage acts and parlour games didn't go quite to plan. So, one day I presented myself, explaining that I was searching for work as I had fallen out with Cotton. Francisco took the bait and hired me on the spot, keen to know all that I could tell him about Cotton's tricks and scams. I played along, but kept Cotton informed.

"Over time, the old man seemed to trust me more and more, revealing all of the details behind his acts. For a while, I shared everything with Cotton, but began to have second thoughts. In my absence, Cotton had begun to rely more and more on Walter, my alcoholic brother. As siblings we had never been close and Walter used the opportunity to poison Cotton against me.

"I began to think that I might be better off sticking with the Faccini family. Francisco had really taken me under his wing, and Angelina and I had become very close. We kept our feelings for each other secret, although we had begun to talk about the possibility of marriage. But all of that ended when Cotton decided to go to the police with the information he now had on his rival. Francisco knew immediately that I must have been the source and I had no option but to fall back in with Cotton and my brother.

"When the trial started, the Italian families had begun to threaten us and, with Francisco's death, Cotton fled to the Continent knowing that his days were numbered. Walter and I were more fortunate, having good contacts in London. We kept out of sight and out of trouble, eventually picking up work for Halvergate."

Holmes interposed at this juncture. "You never told Halvergate about your troubles with the Faccini family did you?"

Spencer looked confused. "No. Walter and I never discussed the matter with anyone. Over time, everyone seemed content to believe that we were just another couple of heavies who had always worked for Halvergate. And as the months rolled by, we wrongly believed that the Italians were only interested in pursuing Cotton. When we heard that George had been stabbed in Lille, it came as no surprise."

This time, it was I who posed a question. "When did you realise that you and Walter were still being pursued?"

Spencer sat down on the wooden chair and took a deep breath. His right elbow rested on the table and he began to cradle his forehead as if in pain. "It was a chance encounter. Walter had taken to drinking in a pub close to Covent Garden. When he was drunk, he would talk, and when he talked he didn't seem to mind who heard. One night, a month or so ago, he began to brag about how he had outwitted the Faccini family. A lot of people heard, including the Italian landlord. I dragged him from the bar, but feared the worse. Yesterday afternoon, as I was stuck in traffic and sat in a cab on Catherine Street, I saw a tall, elegant woman emerge from a passageway to the side of *The Glendower*. She didn't see me, but I realised instantly that it was Angelina.

"I had no idea how quickly the killer might act. And to make matters worse, Walter had disappeared after a lunchtime drinking bout. I realise now that he must have been led to his death by men known to the Faccini family. That evening he was sat at the same bar near Covent Garden with a couple of newfound 'friends' when Angelina walked in. Of course, Walter had never met her, and being drunk was easily fooled into thinking that this very alluring woman was

135

genuinely attracted to him. When she suggested that he walk her back to her guesthouse, Walter was but a lamb to the slaughter.

"I pitched up in the pub about an hour after Walter had left. A friendly face in the bar had seen the pair leave. I knew that meant he was already likely to be dead. There was thick fog in town at that time, but it didn't take me long to find his body in a side street near some discarded boxes. The stiletto knife and card confirmed that the Faccini's had been responsible. As I crouched near his body, I could hear voices and footsteps coming towards me. I tip-toed away, fearing that I too had been seen by the Italians, but as I continued down the passageway, heard a police whistle behind me. I realised that I had not been the first to find the body and the police had clearly been summoned.

"At that stage, I didn't know that Angelina had been responsible for the stabbing and thought only that she had lured Walter to his death at the hands of another assassin. I guessed that she had been staying at the guesthouse I had seen her emerge from earlier that day, so set off to confront her. It wasn't difficult to find the room and having knocked lightly forced my way in through the door when she opened it.

"Angelina was like a caged tiger. Her eyes were wild and she clawed at my face as I pushed her into the room. I slapped her and told her to calm down explaining that I just wanted to know what had happened to Walter and did not blame her for helping someone else to kill him. At that point, she went quiet, took a deep breath and stared at me intently. Then she stepped back, laughed unexpectedly and continued to laugh. At first, it unnerved me, but within a few seconds I realised why she was laughing and moved towards her. She made a lunge towards the bathroom door and flung it open. But I was too quick for her and soon had my hands around her throat. I'm not proud of what I did after that."

Spencer paused and looked to be greatly overcome with emotion. Holmes merely continued with the interrogation: "And having strangled her, you then realised that you had been stabbed?"

"Yes," he replied weakly. "I had not felt the blade at all, but saw the knife as I turned her body over. It was only later that I realised just how deep the wound was."

"And what did you do after that?"

"I left Catherine Street in a cab and made my way to Halvergate's house. It was then close to eleven thirty and he was livid that I had called so late. He was even angrier when I told him what had happened to Walter and how I had killed Angelina Faccini. Despite that, he agreed to help me and told me to make my way here, to the *White Lion*, where Alfie Pitman would take care of me."

Holmes now decided to play Devil's Advocate. "And you believed that, did you?"

"I'm not sure I follow you?"

"Well, has it not occurred to you, how quickly and easily we were able to find you? You must surely realise that it was Halvergate who put us on your trail."

For the first time, Spencer looked at him defiantly. "He wouldn't do that!"

Holmes pulled from his pocket the Halvergate letter and placed it on the table before Spencer. It took him some minutes to absorb the full significance of the communication. When he had done so, he looked up at the two of us. "It seems you were right, Mr Holmes – 'No honour among thieves' as they say."

*************************

We had taken Bill Spencer to the police station at Bow Street later that evening, where he was arrested for the murder of Angelina Faccini. He had put up no resistance and seemed resigned to his fate.

When we arrived back at Baker Street we found Wiggins waiting in the upstairs room. He reported that Inspector Hopkins had been overjoyed to learn of our progress on the case, but was a little bewildered as to how we had gained entry to the room at *The Glendower*. Wiggins had apparently reassured him that we discovered the door unlocked when we first arrived. Holmes showed his appreciation for all that Wiggins had done by opening a prized bottle of single malt and insisting that we drink a toast to the Baker Street Irregulars.

It was a little beyond eleven o'clock the following morning when Inspector Hopkins arrived at 221B. There was no mistaking his elation at the events of the previous day, for at Mrs Hudson's direction he fairly bounded up the seventeen stairs to greet us.

"I am so grateful, gentleman!" he said, being invited to take an armchair. "I was pleased to hear young Wiggins's report yesterday, but imagine my surprise on returning to the station late last night to find Bill Spencer in the cells. A fine piece of detective work, I must confess!"

Holmes brushed aside the praise and focused instead on the precautions Hopkins had taken to protect Spencer from an early death at the hands of a criminal assassin. The Inspector replied confidently: "Rest assured, Mr Holmes. He is alone in a cell under heavy guard and will remain isolated and protected until after his trial."

"That is good to hear. I cannot emphasise enough how dangerous the man's position is. Spencer is content for it to be known publicly that he was responsible for bringing about the deaths of Francisco and Angelina Faccini. He also wants it to be known that in seeking to outwit the Italian families, he and his brother asked Edwin Halvergate for protection and were taken on as criminal associates."

Hopkins looked troubled on hearing this. "That is not altogether true. I understood that Halvergate had been ignorant of Spencer's links to the Faccini family."

"Yes," replied Holmes. "But Spencer wanted to exact some revenge for what Halvergate did in exposing him as a murderer. He therefore wants the information I just imparted to be shared far and wide."

"And just how will he do that from inside a police cell?"

Holmes flashed Hopkins a mischievous grin. "Oh, I don't think he'll need to. As we speak, the Baker Street Irregulars are doing their best to spread the word. By this evening, every criminal in London will believe that Halvergate has played a major role in seeking to undermine the Italian families."

Hopkins continued to look sternly at Holmes. "Then, I hope you know what you are doing? Halvergate will soon work out that you are the real architect of this plan."

"Indeed, my friend. That is the intention. '...Cry 'Havoc!' and let slip the dogs of war...' He will be forced to break cover now and when he does, Watson and I will be waiting for him."

It was a bold and risky move on my friend's part and one that was to have far-reaching implications for both of us in the month that followed. When Hopkins had left, Holmes reached for his briar pipe and stared into the fire before adding simply, "'Beware the Ides of March...'"

# 7. The Mile End Mynah Bird

In the winter of 1919 there remained a general air of despondency in Britain with the interminable upheavals caused by the aftermath of the Great War. While there had been widespread jubilation at the end of the conflict, the mood of the population had soured with the slow demobilisation of troops from the western front and the influenza pandemic that had continued to sweep across Europe claiming hundreds of thousands of lives. In the previous month, there had been around a thousand deaths in London alone and with the significant shortage of medical personnel to cope with such demands, I had felt it my duty to come out of retirement and assist where I could. By day, I attended a number of patients on a private basis, while three nights a week I acted as an unpaid consultant at the Charing Cross Hospital just off The Strand.

I was on duty one evening when a young man was rushed in to the emergency ward of the hospital on an orderly's trolley. The police officer who accompanied him explained breathlessly that the patient had been shot, the result, he said, of what looked like an attempted murder. As fortune would have it, the shoulder wound sustained by the man looked worse than it was, the bullet having passed across the top of his collar bone. With some minor surgery we had the patient patched up and sedated for the night within a couple of hours, just before I finished my shift at ten o'clock.

Police Constable Dunning had continued to wait for news of the patient and when his charge had been transferred to a bed in a quiet side ward of the hospital, had pulled up a chair alongside the sleeping man. Dunning was a tall, fair-haired

Scot, with broad cheek bones and exceptionally large hands. He explained that his divisional inspector had ordered him to stay with the injured man as a measure of protection. Curious to know why the metropolitan force was taking such precautions, I asked him who the patient was.

"He told us his name was Jonathon Christie. Beyond that, we know nothing of the man. It was the only information he was prepared to share with us, Doctor."

"Then why the heavy-handed police presence?" I queried.

"The man who shot him was Serang Sayan, a lascar sailor. He is wanted in connection with a number of assaults which we believe he carried out with his brother, Bhandarry, under the direction of an East End moneylender named Sydney Vulliamy."

"...And both Vulliamy and Bhandarry Sayan appear to have disappeared, PC Dunning. Neither has been seen for over three weeks, according to my sources..."

Both Dunning and I turned sharply towards the door as the voice came from behind us, my own senses heightened immediately by the familiar timbre. "Holmes!" I cried. "What brings you here?"

"I might ask you the same, Watson, but your attire speaks for itself. Not quite the relaxed retirement you had in mind, I'd warrant."

Dunning looked from Holmes towards me with evident glee. "Dr Watson! I'm so sorry, sir, I hadn't realised from our earlier conversations that you were *the* 'Dr Watson'. Mr Holmes has been with us for the past month. It has been an honour to work with him and now I've finally got to meet you as well."

I smiled at him and then nodded affectionately towards Holmes: "Not much of a retirement for you either, then?"

"No, just can't keep out of trouble. But it's good to see you, Watson. It must be a good six months since we last spoke."

We chatted along for a few minutes, catching up on all that had happened, relaxed in each other's company and almost oblivious to the presence of PC Dunning, who sat quietly by the hospital bed. At sixty-five, Holmes retained a youthful look, his dark hair swept back and showing only a fringe of grey at the temples, his eyes still bright and alert. He stood tall in a fawn-coloured Norfolk jacket with matching waistcoat and trousers and light-brown brogues.

We moved on to the subject of the shooting. Holmes explained that he had been given a short briefing on the events earlier that evening, but asked Dunning to provide his own account. The officer was pleased to oblige: "About six-thirty, we received a telephone call from a Mr Metcalf, the landlord of the *Bancroft Arms* on the Mile End Road. He said that a scuffle had taken place in the tap room of the bar and a man had been shot. The gunman had been prevented from leaving the bar by some of the pub regulars, who had taken the small pistol from him. They held him prisoner until we arrived about half an hour later.

"I accompanied Inspector Banns and PC Moxon. When we got there, the Inspector and I were delighted to see that the man being pinned to the ground by three hefty drinkers was Serang Sayan."

Holmes nodded while Dunning paused and gestured towards Christie. "This young fellow lay face down on the floor of the tap room. We thought he was dead at first, but when we turned him over could see that he was still breathing. He looked to have been shot in the shoulder at close range by the Derringer pistol and was probably knocked unconscious as he fell to the floor. Sayan clearly thought he'd killed him, for when the Inspector asked the publican for some smelling salts and brought Christie around a short while later, the sailor made a wild lunge at him. Before we separated them, Sayan glared at Christie, held a forefinger to his own lips and then ran it across his throat."

"As if telling Christie to keep quiet or face the consequences?"

"Yes, Doctor, that is what we believe. And it seems it had the desired effect. Christie would only tell us his name and refused to say anything further about the attempt on his life."

At this, Holmes expressed some surprise. "He has said nothing at all beyond that?"

"No, Mr Holmes. Well, actually, he did say *one* other thing, although it didn't seem that significant. He said: 'Please take care of Delilah'."

"And you have no idea to whom he may have been referring?"

"No, sir. He has been silent ever since. Inspector Banns and PC Moxon left to take Sayan to a nearby lock-up and I was instructed to wait for the ambulance and to stay with Christie until told otherwise."

"I see. Well, the bad news is that Sayan has managed to escape. Inspector Banns left him at the lock-up in the charge of a constable who was evidently duped. Apparently, Sayan fell to the floor of the cell, shaking violently and foaming at the mouth. The constable unlocked the door, believing him to be suffering some sort of fit and was immediately set upon by our man, who escaped and was last seen heading along Hanbury Street. Banns has alerted all divisions to keep an eye out and, despite all of the yuletide demands on the force, is confident that Sayan will be retaken. In the meantime, he has asked me to look into Christie's affairs and see if I can make sense of what has gone on and how it might relate to our wider investigations into the activities of Vulliamy, the moneylender."

"Is this moneylender dangerous then, Holmes?" I enquired.

"Yes, he set up his money making venture in the East End about three years ago. Those who fall foul of him and fail to repay their loans, and the exorbitant rates of interest he charges, have been subjected to threats and assaults, perpetrated by his loyal sidekicks, Serang and Bhandarry Sayan. The Hindu brothers have gained some notoriety for their barbaric methods of extracting money from those in debt to Vulliamy.

"So far, the gang has managed to stay one step ahead of Inspector Banns's men who were tasked with shutting down the moneylending operation. Scotland Yard fears that Vulliamy is being protected by a high-ranking officer within the force who is receiving bribes in return for intelligence on the unfolding police investigation. The Commissioner, Sir Nevil Macready, asked me a month or so back if I could provide some assistance. As yet, I have seen no evidence of police corruption in the case, but believe that Sidney Vulliamy and Bhandarry Sayan are lying low in the knowledge that we are investigating their affairs."

PC Dunning then asked, "Do you think it possible that Serang Sayan might come here and try to finish Christie, Mr Holmes?"

My colleague answered him directly. "No. I think that very unlikely. Clearly, you will need to be on your guard, but I suspect our sailor will be long gone."

Dunning look relieved. Holmes then probed whether the Constable had taken time to search Christie at any point. Dunning shifted uneasily and admitted that he had not. It was then that I remembered Christie's grey woollen jacket in the operating theatre.

"Actually, Holmes, I had to cut the jacket from Christie before we could patch up his shoulder. I asked one of the orderlies to package it up along with his boots and a necklace and place them in one of the lockers outside the theatre. I could go and retrieve the package, if you think it important?"

Holmes beamed. "Excellent. That would be most helpful."

When I returned to the side ward, Holmes was sat on a chair on the opposite side of the bed to PC Dunning looking intently at the patient. He was puffing away on a pipe, the strong tobacco smoke mingling with the smell of surgical spirit and reminding me of happier days in the upstairs room of our Baker Street apartment.

"You know, I should tell you to take that pipe outside the ward, Holmes," I said with a broad smirk. "The hospital takes a dim view of smokers on surgical wards these days."

Holmes looked at me absentmindedly and then removed the pipe from his mouth. "Apologies, Doctor. Old habits die hard, as they say."

I passed him the package. He removed the string, undid the bundle and placed the brown paper on the floor. One sleeve of the grey jacket lay on top of the garment, the result of my earlier work with the scalpel. Holmes glanced over it, and then dropped it onto the brown paper. Lifting the rest of the jacket he then began his detailed examination; smelling the woollen fibres, checking all of the pockets, removing a couple of items and scrutinising every point of interest with his familiar magnifying glass. When he had finished, he turned his attention to the necklace which also lay on top of the jacket, and then the footwear; a pair of scuffed black leather ankle boots which had clearly seen better days. It had been some time since I had seen him in action and I was every bit as fascinated as PC Dunning to watch the consulting detective at work.

After what seemed like an age, Holmes looked up and spoke. "Not much to be gathered, but a few pointers which may be useful. Christie is an apprentice stonemason, left-handed and twenty-two years of age. He lives in a modest house in Mile End Old Town and is a keen gardener. He also has a nervous disposition, which may be the result of a recent loss, and is a devout Anglican and pacifist."

Dunning chortled. "Mr Holmes, you are truly remarkable. How any man could presume to know so much, from so little, is beyond me."

I recognised the hint of irritation which passed momentarily across my colleague's face. "Constable, if you had searched Christie you would have been able to discern much of this. He wears a St Christopher's medallion, a clear sign of his faith. On the back there are two separate pieces of engraving. The first is his name and date of birth, probably done when he was given the medal as a child – the engraving being difficult to pick out given the wear on the silver. A much more recent engraving displays the name 'Benjamin Christie' and a date of '2nd November 1919'. It suggests the very recent death of a family member - a father, brother or uncle, perhaps - which may account for his nervousness. His nails are ragged and bitten to the quick and yet this is not a long-standing habit, for he has well-formed cuticles.

"In his pocket is a three-year old document which announces his official status as a 'conscientious objector'. It tells us that he was successful at his wartime tribunal in seeking to be excused from bearing arms, but was required to undertake some trade or profession in support of the war effort – clear proof of his pacifism and again suggestive of a strong religious conviction. The document also identifies his address on 'Louisa Street', about half a mile from the *Bancroft Arms*. I know the area. It is a road of well-appointed terraced houses which have small gardens to their rear and is a refuge for many tradesmen and professionals of the middling order."

"But how do you know Christie is a stonemason - and an apprentice at that?" quizzed Dunning.

"A close examination of the fibres on his jacket reveals evidence of a fine white dust, unmistakably tiny fragments of Portland stone. His left hand bears the scars of his profession; the hard skin on the fingertips, the engrained dust on the palm and a slight swelling around each of the knuckles. In muscular terms, his right arm is the more fully developed - confirmation that it is used to wield a stonemason's mallet. At twenty-two he is unlikely to be a master stonemason, so alongside the other discernible facts I would suggest that he is still completing his apprenticeship. And if I had to be pushed on the nature of his work as a non-combatant during the war, I would submit that he was most likely engaged in preparing tombstones and memorial plaques for those who died fighting on foreign soil."

PC Dunning looked on in awe. Holmes concluded his deposition with a few final words: "As for the gardening, the underside of his boots testifies to the frequent use of a spade.

There are clear ridges on the left hand sole where the ball of the foot has been used to tread down on the spade. The ridges are absent from the other sole. We know that his house has a garden. I would expect it to be well-tended."

"Bravo!" said I. "And what do you propose to do now, having learned so much about our mystery man?"

"Why, visit his home, of course. There is no time like the present, my friend."

"Splendid. I have just finished my shift, so if you have no objection, Holmes, I would be pleased to accompany you."

PC Dunning looked crestfallen. "I wish I could join you, gentlemen, but duty compels me to stay here until I am relieved by PC Moxon. Good luck with your endeavours."

************************

It was surprisingly mild that evening as we walked out onto The Strand in search of a taxi. There was a strong and welcome aroma of ground coffee in the air from one of the many cafés that had sprung up now that the war had ended. While it was busy on the thoroughfare, it took us little time to find a taxi rank and a cabbie willing to drive us the three miles into Mile End Old Town.

Sat in the back of the taxi, Holmes announced suddenly that he had not been entirely honest with PC Dunning. "There are some features to this case which are, for the moment, somewhat baffling, Watson. I did not wish to set hares coursing by mentioning it, but it was clear to me that Christie had gone in to that pub for a specific reason. He is no drinker. In fact, in an inside pocket of his jacket was a signed 'pledge' in support of his abstinence. Close to it was another item I failed to point out to Dunning – a sheathed hunting knife made by J B Schofield of Sheffield. Hardly the sort of weapon we might expect a pacifist to be carrying. Until I am in possession of some further data which may shed light on these apparent anomalies, I would prefer to keep the matters from the police."

"Understood, Holmes – as you wish."

It was a little after eleven o'clock when we alighted from the taxi at the entrance to Louisa Street. The gas lamps along the street cast a warm glow on the yellow brick terraced houses, which were nicely proportioned with a front entrance door, single downstairs window and two upper sash windows comprised of six over six panelled glass panes. Christie's property was some way along the street to our right. Unlike many of the homes nearby, it appeared to have no Christmas decorations on view. Just before we reached it, Holmes whispered that we should be discreet in our business. I noted that he had already withdrawn from his pocket a set of keys.

"A stroke of luck, Watson – a standard Davenport rim lock," he said in a hushed tone. His fingers worked quickly as he sought out the correct skeleton key and inserted it in the lock. With a faint click the lock was undone and Holmes turned the doorknob. We wasted no time in entering the house and closing the door behind us.

For a few seconds we stood in darkness. I heard Holmes returning the set of keys to his pocket and then saw a slim shaft of light stretching out before us and illuminating the narrow hallway of the house. Holmes held in his hand a small silver canister, from which the light was emanating.

"A new toy?" I whispered.

"Yes, indeed - a Winchester pocket flashlight. A small gift from a grateful American client. It is powered by two small electric batteries. I wouldn't be without it."

On the right, a short distance along the hallway was a closed door. Holmes opened it and we stepped into the room to find that it was the front parlour. Illuminated by a gas lamp across the street and the more telling beams from the flashlight, it looked to be sparsely yet luxuriously furnished, the wallpaper a dark red colour with an intricate floral pattern. Either side of a small fireplace and hearth on the opposite wall there were tall mahogany bookshelves filled with volumes of all sizes. Set in the far corner against the window was a small green leather armchair with an accompanying side table. It was the full extent of the furniture.

"Mr Christie is clearly a man of modest means," I ventured.

"You forget that he is still completing his apprenticeship. This is a desirable property for someone of his age and profession. I would venture that he inherited the house from his parents and until recently lived here with an older brother."

I expressed some surprise. "Why do you say that?"

"The décor is too florid and fussy for a working man in his early twenties. On the mantelpiece is a photograph of an older couple and beside it another of two dark-haired men, unquestionably brothers, the younger looking of which is Jonathon Christie."

"...With the other being the recently deceased 'Benjamin Christie'?"

"My thoughts exactly," chimed Holmes.

As we were about to step out of the parlour and back into the hallway, there was a loud shriek from elsewhere within the house. We both froze, the beam from the flashlight playing out into the empty hall and giving us no clue as to the identity of the screamer. A chilling voice then uttered: "I'll kill him! I'll kill him!"

Holmes strode out of the room and passed quickly along the hallway. I followed behind, noting a stairwell to our right, as we entered the main downstairs room of the property. In the uncertain light, we relied on the flashlight to make sense of what now lay before us: a mirror on one wall; a large table in a corner on which sat a piece of white stone; another bookshelf; and a couple of wooden dining chairs. A space no bigger than fifteen feet square with a window directly ahead of us and a further closed door to the right. And yet nowhere within the space could we see any human form. As my eyes began to scan around the floor for anyone lurking near the wainscot, the same screeching voice echoed around the room: "Two down and one across! Two down and one across!"

The next noise came from Holmes, who broke suddenly into an uncontrolled chuckle and guffaw. It left me with a discomforting sense of bewilderment. *What exactly was going on?*

My gaze followed the beam of his flashlight into the corner of the room to our right. It was then that I saw the reason for his mirth. Hanging from a chain, on a hook fastened into the ceiling, was a cage some three or four feet in diameter in which I could see perched a striking, stocky-looking bird of oriental appearance. The blue-black sheen of its feathers was tinged with a purple hue and I could see distinct bright orange patches along its wings. In contrast, the legs and bill of the specimen were a bright yellow and it was around ten inches in height.

"My God, Holmes! It's a damned parrot!"

"Hardly - this bird is something far more impressive. You are looking at a Mynah bird, a creature which can imitate the human voice." He moved closer, angling the beam of the torch away from the cage, so as not to shine the light directly into the bird's eyes. "A most remarkable specimen, eh? And another mystery solved..."

"Yes. I'm thinking that this must be Christie's 'Delilah'?"

The Mynah bird seemed to chirp in confirmation.

"It seems we all concur!" laughed Holmes. "And I'm pleased to note that the ravages of war and early retirement have not dulled your senses, Watson. Now, let's see what other clues we can find."

It was good to be back at his side. I had quite forgotten just how much I had missed Holmes and the adventures we had shared for so many years. He seemed to be in fine fettle and having scanned the rest of the room with the flashlight, walked across to examine the white stone on the large corner table.

"This is very nearly completed - a grave marker, no less. But why would Christie work on this at home, rather than at work? He seems to have fashioned it here on this very table, with just a few basic tools." His hands worked their way around the stone cross, touching its contours, feeling the fine dust which covered each surface. "I may not be a master stonemason, but this looks like a pretty basic piece of work, with little finesse. I would say that Christie produced this at some speed and with little enthusiasm."

"Perhaps he picks up the odd private commission, outside of his day to day work, to earn a bit of extra money?" I suggested.

"Hmm...Possibly."

"Two down and one across! Two down and one across!" Delilah's piercing squawk filled the room once more.

"Is it conceivable that our rare avian has a penchant for those strange word puzzles that you used to delight in, Holmes?" The comment was made in jest, but my colleague responded positively.

"That is not so far-fetched. You may remember that the first 'word cross' puzzle appeared in the *New York World* five or six years ago - the invention of a Mr Arthur Wynne, a journalist originally from Liverpool, I believe. Since that time a number of American newspapers have included daily or weekly 'crossword puzzles' within their pages. I confess that I still find them diverting in the absence of any other mental stimulation. It is possible that Christie enjoyed the same leisurely pursuit, although it's hard to imagine him shouting out the elements of a puzzle he may have been struggling with."

"Yes, I fancy that the bird will only remember and repeat short phrases which are said over and over again."

"I'll kill him! I'll kill him!" shrieked the Mynah.

"Indeed," mused Holmes, his eyes narrowing as he scrutinised the bird afresh, "how true."

Our continued investigation of the downstairs living room threw up no further clues. Beyond the room was a small kitchen, again sparsely furnished, with a small side door from it leading to the rear garden of the property. The set of skeleton keys again proved useful.

In the narrow beam of the flashlight we stepped quietly outside the back door and into a short passage which ran along the length of the kitchen. To our left was the wall of the neighbouring property. Beyond the passageway, paved slabs, laid end to end, ran down the length of the garden to the left, ending in a wide gate set within a wall at the bottom. To the right of this I could just make out a small wooden shed. The remainder of the land was given over to soil, most of which had been overtaken by weeds. The garden was flanked on both sides by tall brick walls, shielding us from view.

Holmes edged forward in small steps doing his best to examine all areas of the garden in the uncertain light. I tucked myself in behind him so as not to impede his progress.

Two-thirds of the way down the garden he paused and turned to me, whispering: "This patch of earth has been dug recently. But the rest is something of a mess. Christie may be less of a gardener than I imagined." I nodded in agreement, noting a spade, still upright, in the soil beside a long open trench.

When we had reached the end of the garden, Holmes spent some time looking in through the window of the wooden shed. He held the flashlight above his head and played its beam down at an angle into every part of the interior, standing on tip-toes at one point to ensure that he had seen everything he could from his vantage point. With a quick look over the smokehouse lock on the outside of the door, he had apparently seen everything he needed to.

Before returning to the house, Holmes spent some minutes examining the paving slabs and soil close to the green-painted garden gate. With some excitement, he pointed down at a number of distinct muddy tracks on the first half dozen paving slabs. I nodded again in confirmation as he brought the torchlight up to see my reaction. I had seen the tracks, but had no idea why Holmes felt them to be so significant. I

It was only when we were back in the kitchen and he had successfully relocked the rear door that we began to speak. I followed him through to the living room, where he lit a candle on the table and switched off the flashlight.

"Well, what do you make of it all? Casts a new light on the case, don't you think?" I had to confess to being none the wiser. "I'm sorry, Holmes. I did see the tracks you pointed to near the gate and the recently dug earth. I also saw the contents of the shed – a few tools hanging on the rear wall and the painted boards and advertising signs stacked up on the floor nearby. But I have no clear idea what it tells us."

"What did you see *on the signs*?" asked Holmes.

"Some painted pictures of fruit and vegetables and some prices for various produce."

"Precisely – you saw everything I did and yet you seem not to have grasped its significance. Christie is clearly a stonemason as we suspected. However, it seems reasonable to conclude that his recently deceased brother was a greengrocer, who plied his trade from a hand cart. The signs and track marks tell us as much."

I felt a tad slighted. "Well I saw no hand cart. How do you explain that?"

"That is a lead which we have yet to follow. But you cannot doubt that a hand cart was involved. You saw the tracks yourself. A larger vehicle would not have fitted through the gate."

"Granted. But what significance does this have for the case and the attack on Christie?"

"Two down and one across!" It was Delilah, reminding us of her presence in the corner of the room.

Holmes smirked. "That clever bird has just given you the answer, my friend."

"No, I don't see it at all."

"Cast your mind back. Sidney Vulliamy and Bhandarry Sayan appear to have disappeared. Serang Sayan had attempted to kill Christie. It is possible that the two acts are linked. Let us suppose that Christie wished to kill the moneylender."

"Hence the Mynah's repeated call: 'I'll kill him! I'll kill him!"

"Exactly," replied Holmes. "Christie is a man of faith, a teetotaller and a pacifist. A resort to violence would not ordinarily be part of his *modus operandi* and yet we find him carrying a hunting knife and involved in an altercation with a violent offender in a public house a few days before one of the most significant events in the Christian calendar. Serang Sayan does not usually resort to firearms. The attacks he has carried out for Sidney Vulliamy have been vicious, but he has always stopped short of murder. Why is he also acting out of character?"

"You suspect this has something to do with Christie's older brother?"

"Yes – that is the key to this. It cannot have been easy trying to eke out a living as a greengrocer, with all of the deprivations that we continue to experience here in London, despite the end of the war. It is not fanciful to imagine that the man may have found himself in debt, paying over the odds for a limited supply of fresh produce, while his customers struggle to find the cash to pay for the fruit and vegetables he has on display. In desperation, he is reluctant to fall back on the limited earnings of his beloved younger brother, so turns instead to Vulliamy, the local moneylender. From there it is a slippery slope into debt and the unwanted attentions of the Sayan brothers."

At last I could see where he was heading. "So you believe that they murdered the greengrocer and Christie has been seeking to exact his revenge?"

"That is possible, although it is more likely that their heavy handed tactics led to his suicide. Either way, I do believe that they were responsible for his death and Christie has indeed been out for revenge – with some success, I have to say."

"I'm not sure I follow."

"Come on, Watson! You must know where this is leading. I was right to suggest that Christie has been doing lots of digging recently, but a look at the back yard tells us he is clearly no gardener. If I am not mistaken, that freshly-dug section of earth towards the end of the garden is now the resting place of Sidney Vulliamy and Bhandarry Sayan. He murdered them and transported their bodies here using the greengrocer's cart. It was the perfect way to move them without attracting attention."

My surprise was palpable. "Really – how can you be so sure?"

He turned towards the bird cage. "It was Delilah here that confirmed the matter. She is well named. Was it not Delilah, a woman in the valley of Sorek, who betrayed Samson in the *Book of Judges*? This Mynah bird has done the same for young Christie. Not only has she told us of the man's deep-seated hatred of Vulliamy and his intentions to '...kill him!', but has provided us with testimony on Christie's thoughts after the murders. The bird can be forgiven for misquoting the stonemason. 'Two down and one across!' was no reference to a crossword clue. What Christie actually said was, 'Two down and *for one a cross*! Meaning that he had despatched two of the three men he sought and felt obliged to provide a Christian burial for Vulliamy."

"The crudely carved stone cross which sits on the table here!" I added. "Perhaps he believed that as a Hindu, Bhandarry Sayan would not require the same treatment."

"That is my supposition."

"And the confrontation in the *Bancroft Arms* – was that Christie's attempt to assassinate the last of the trio?"

"No, unlikely, I would say. It seems more plausible that Serang was pursuing Christie, in the full knowledge that the stonemason had murdered Bhandarry and Vulliamy. He was carrying a loaded gun after all. Christie would not ordinarily have gone into a public house. I believe he entered the establishment in fear of his life, having been chased by Serang. That working hypothesis also helps to explain why Christie has, so far, been tight-lipped about the whole affair."

"He is fearful of being exposed as a double murderer!"

"Yes – the lascar's finger across the throat gesture seems to confirm that. He was telling Christie to hold his tongue. Serang will stop at nothing to avenge the death of his brother, but he will not risk involving the police. He has too much to lose. We must be wary, Watson. This man is extremely dangerous. It is not the first time we have faced such an adversary. You might remember the lascar sailor we encountered in the case you so lovingly embellished as *The Man with the Twisted Lip*."

Had it not been for the wry smile that accompanied his words, I might have taken the remark as a criticism, but knew that not to be the case. I ignored the taunt and turned instead to our plan of action: "Where do we go from here?"

"I have a suite at the Grosvenor Hotel in Victoria. There is more than enough space for the two of us. I suggest we take advantage of a decent meal and a good night's sleep and then set out first thing tomorrow to track down our elusive sailor."

I was taken aback. "Really - is there not a case for acting while the iron is hot, so to speak?"

"Serang Sayan is going nowhere, my friend. He has half the metropolitan force out looking for him, an East Bengal sailor far from home. I know exactly where he will be hiding and it will not hurt to keep our powder dry for a dawn assault."

With that, he extinguished the candle and resorted once more to the flashlight. As he reached the door of the living room, he turned to me and nodded towards the corner of the room. "Don't forget Delilah, Watson! We can't leave the poor creature here, especially as she has been so helpful in our enquiries!"

***********************

It was close to five-thirty the next morning when I was woken rather sharply by Holmes in the luxurious surroundings of the Grosvenor Hotel. Our arrival the previous night had sparked a considerable flurry of activity. Holmes had left the Mynah in the care of a bemused night porter with full instructions to ensure that the bird was fed and watered and properly accommodated. The concierge had arranged for a bed to be made up for me within Holmes's suite and some ten minutes later a plate of sandwiches and a bottle of Burgundy had arrived in the room. It has been sometime since I had enjoyed such extravagance.

"Good morning, my dear fellow! I trust that you slept well? A maid has just returned your shirt, washed and ironed, and these trousers have been pressed to within an inch of their lives! I took the liberty of ordering room service - a small cooked breakfast to help us on our way."

My response was heartfelt. "Holmes, it is a pleasure to be back in your company. While it seems slightly bizarre to be investigating grim murder at such a festive time, I cannot tell you how much I have missed our adventures together."

I could see that my comments had touched him, but he turned away, avoiding my gaze, busying himself with the tray of breakfast items and the large silver coffee pot at its centre. Our conversation thereafter was focused on the case.

Evidently, Holmes had been busy during the few hours that I slumbered. He told me that he had managed to reach Inspector Banns by telephone a short while earlier and had arranged for a team of detectives to meet us later that morning at a point of rendezvous. He had also pinpointed the location where he believed Serang Sayan would be hiding.

I expressed my disbelief at this rapid rate of progress. "How on earth did you manage to find the hideout without leaving the hotel?"

"Eyes and ears! You remember the old days when we made good use of the Baker Street Irregulars, that proud group of itinerant ragamuffins that I valued so highly. Well, while the Irregulars are long gone, their erstwhile leader, the indomitable Charlie Wiggins, has always stayed in touch and prior to the war ran a successful business as a private investigator. Having been called up for war service, he has now returned to London, keen to resume the profession. This is the first opportunity I have had to involve him in a case and he has clearly lost none of his talents. I called him by telephone last night and set him to work. Only half an hour ago he rang back to say that his discreet enquiries had enabled him to locate the hideout close to the Mile End Road."

"But how did he know which area to concentrate on? You cannot tell me he has the ability to search the whole of London in one night?"

"No – but it was clear that the search would be more limited. Our hypothesis was that Christie's brother had worked as a greengrocer using a hand cart, and that Christie had used the cart to transport the dead bodies back to Louisa Street. The tracks on the garden path indicated that more than one journey had been made. I therefore concluded that he moved the bodies one at a time."

"I see. So you were working on the basis that with the weight of the bodies, Christie had travelled a relatively short distance?"

"You have it in one. I told Wiggins to focus his attention on the streets close to Christie's home. He found what he was looking for on White Horse Lane."

"And what was he looking for?"

"The missing cart. Having taken the second of the bodies back to Louisa Street, I believe that Christie returned to the murder scene a final time. The more I thought about it last night, the more convinced I was that he would only have done that for one reason."

"Which was?"

"To collect a third body to fill that one remaining trench in the garden. I believe that he thought he had killed all three men and was returning for Serang Sayan. However, when he got there he found that the lascar was still alive and waiting for him. Christie flees, leaving the cart and is pursued by

Serang. He tries to escape into the *Bancroft Arms* and is shot by the sailor and left for dead."

"It sounds remarkable, but fits the facts as we know them. And if Wiggins has found the cart at the hideout, it lends further credence to your theory."

"Indeed. And with our breakfast finished, we can now put our theory to the test."

It was just past seven-fifteen that morning when our taxi dropped us off at a quiet location along White Horse Lane. Waiting there was Inspector Banns and six uniformed constables, all armed, we were told, with standard issue Webley revolvers. Holmes quickly briefed the men on what we had found out and Banns confirmed that he knew exactly where to find the hideout. Some minutes later the police had the three-storey brown brick building surrounded. Holmes and I stood at a safe distance across the street watching the drama unfold.

At a given signal, two of the officers were sent to the rear of the house to affect an entrance. Less than a minute later we saw a man stagger from the front door of the dwelling. He had not reached the gate of the front garden when he was brought down in a rugby-style tackle by one of the larger constables. The officer retained his grip and kept the sailor pinned to the floor until the others came to his assistance.

Inspector Banns seemed delighted with the arrest, having said earlier that he feared Serang might be in possession of another firearm. But as the officers searched the prisoner he was found to be carrying only a short knife, some three or four inches in length. The man was no taller than five feet in height, but looked extremely strong and muscular. His bright penetrating eyes fixed on Holmes as we approached the officers, a look nothing short of pure hatred. Holmes smiled back at him, impervious, it seemed, to any threat the man posed. The prisoner then seemed to shake violently and vomited at the feet of one of the constables.

Banns stepped aside from the others and shook us both by the hand. "Thank you, gentleman, I forgot to mention it earlier, but it seems you were right about the garden in Louisa Street. I sent two men there immediately after your telephone call this morning, Mr Holmes. Two bodies were uncovered, and a pathologist is now at the scene. He tells me that there are no obvious signs of violence on either man. So it seems we have some further questions to ask of Jonathon Christie."

"I wonder, in that case, Inspector, if you would permit the two of us to have a short interview with the man, before your formal interrogation. It may help to prepare the ground for you if he knows that the police are already aware of the crime he has committed."

Banns narrowed his eyes slightly while looking at Holmes and then cast a quick glance in my direction. "I'm sure that would not be a problem, sir. You have been invaluable on this investigation and I trust your integrity. Christie is now out of hospital and currently detained in Bow Street police station. I will make the arrangements as soon as I return to the station. Would two o'clock this afternoon be soon enough?"

"That would be perfect," replied Holmes. "I am very grateful to you."

********************

I left Holmes shortly afterwards to return home and attend to one of my private patients. He appeared to be on the mend and imbued with more than a little festive spirit, insisting that I accept a plump turkey from him as some recompense for the many days I had spent nursing him back to health. The consultation lasted about an hour and after preparing a light luncheon and catching up on some correspondence made my way to Bow Street. Holmes was pacing up and down in the lobby of the building when I arrived.

"Is everything alright?" I asked, concerned by the look on his face.

"Yes – just a few odds and ends I cannot fathom. Christie seems curiously ill-named. One wonders how he could have countenanced multiple-murder at this time of year given his apparent faith. I have had a subsequent telephone conversation with Inspector Banns. He tells me that Serang Sayan has been admitted to the Royal Free Hospital suffering from severe stomach pains. As yet, they are unsure whether this is another ruse on his part, but Banns is taking no chances and has two armed officers sat beside his hospital bed. I believe he is genuinely ill and may well have been on the earlier occasion when he escaped custody."

"What makes you say that?"

"Firstly, that I find it hard to imagine he could have faked the foaming at the mouth stunt. And secondly, I have been considering how Christie - a small man not given to violence - managed to overpower three vicious men armed only with a hunting knife. He must have been convinced that he had killed all three to have the confidence to move their bodies one by one in the grocer's cart. And yet, the bodies of Vulliamy and Bhandarry showed no signs of violence. The only plausible explanation is that a powerful gas or poison was involved – one that was administered by Christie himself."

A few minutes later, we were seated in a large ground floor interview room facing Jonathon Christie. He was still heavily bandaged around his upper body, but the colour had returned to his face. The stonemason was the first to talk. "I understand that one of you is Dr Watson, the surgeon who operated on me last night?"

"Yes," I replied, "that's me."

"I just wanted to say how grateful I am for your assistance, Doctor. I genuinely believed that I was going to die as the pain in my shoulder was excruciating."

"In the scheme of things, a routine piece of minor surgery – I have seen much, much worse in recent times, Mr Christie."

My veiled allusion to some of the wartime casualties I had dealt with was clearly not lost on Christie. "Yes, I cannot begin to imagine how anyone coped with the carnage of the Great War. It left many scars."

"Like those on your brother Benjamin?" Holmes's question bypassed any pretence of courtesy and hit Christie hard, just as my colleague had intended.

Christie took a second or two to readjust before responding. "I have, of course, heard of you, Mr Holmes, and read many of the good Doctor's tales of your adventures. Meeting you under these circumstances does not seem quite so inspiring. I imagine you already know every facet of this case and have come here to present your deductions in a theatrical denouement designed to pamper your ego and send me to the gallows."

Holmes appeared to take no offence from the remark and responded with admirable composure. "On the contrary, Mr Christie, Watson and I have made good progress in piecing together various leads and observable facts, but we are still unclear on a number of significant details. We know that you are a man of faith who has struggled with his conscience since the death of your brother. We believe you set out to murder the three men you blamed for his death - Vulliamy, the moneylender, and his two accomplices, Serang and Bhandarry Sayan. My supposition is that you gassed or poisoned all three men and then sought to bury their bodies in your back garden. Had it not been for Serang Sayan, who clearly survived the poisoning, you may well have succeeded. In the event, when you returned to White Horse Lane for the third time, you found him alive and out for revenge. He chased you along the Mile End Road and into the *Bancroft Arms* where he then shot you. Until the police arrived, he was convinced you were dead, and having realised that you were not, gestured for you to say nothing about the events that had led to the attack."

"That is accurate in every respect. Although I am still bewildered as to why he should have wished for both of us to remain silent."

Holmes nodded. "Serang operates according to an ancient criminal code. He would rather go to his death than inform on another law breaker. He also believes in a tenet that you may now share, namely, 'an eye for an eye'. He will stop at nothing to avenge the death of his brother."

"Then we are not so different after all. As brothers, Benjamin and I were raised in a devoutly Christian family. He held firm to his faith, as did I, but found it increasingly difficult to adhere to the strict pacifist ideals of my parents. When war was declared, he announced that he was enlisting to fight overseas and within weeks left us for his regiment. My father died soon afterwards, and my mother a year later. I was left to run Benjamin's greengrocer's stall until I faced the call-up.

"I thought long and hard about my decision, but applied for conscientious objector status and then appeared before a tribunal. I was granted an exemption from bearing arms but told that I would have to take up a trade or profession in support of the war effort. With the grocery business struggling to pay its way, I enrolled as an apprentice stonemason. It was tough living alone and making ends meet, but I survived until Benjamin returned home in 1917. He was suffering from shellshock and spent six months recovering.

"Having little else to support us, I continued with my apprenticeship and Benjamin did what he could to resurrect the greengrocery business. Within a couple of weeks it was clear that it was never going to provide us with a reliable income and Benjamin began to drink heavily, spending whatever meagre earnings he had made. I did not feel I could voice any objection as I felt like a fraudster, having stayed at home, refusing to enlist.

Sidney Vulliamy had been at school with my brother, although it would be stretching it to say that they had ever been friends. But in need of a few pounds and developing an expensive taste for alcohol, Benjamin turned to the moneylender. Vulliamy was only too happy to assist, spending time drinking with Benjamin and showering him with gifts – one of which 'Delilah', the Mynah bird, who had originally belonged to Bhandarry Sayan.

"It took some time for Benjamin to realise he had been deceived and that all of the money he had been lent would need to be paid back in short-order, along with a considerable sum of interest. Unwilling to saddle me with his debts and terrified about what the Sayan brothers would do given his obvious inability to pay, Benjamin took his life. For once, I was not prepared to sit back and turn the other cheek.

"I knew enough about Vulliamy's business to realise that he operated out of the White Horse Lane address. I also recognised that I would stand no chance of fighting all three men if it came to violence. So I hatched a different plan. I found it was surprisingly easy and cheap to buy tartar emetic over the counter. I purchased small amounts from chemists all over the Capital, so as not to attract attention. The yellow crystals seemed to dissolve easily in alcohol, which I hoped would also mask any taste it had. Knowing the three to be keen drinkers, I mixed a large quantity of the antimony with decent Scotch and then arranged to meet them in White Horse Lane.

"Vulliamy welcomed me into the house, saying how upset he had been to learn of Benjamin's suicide. It was all I could do not to attack him with the hunting knife I had hidden in my pocket. But I was not to be outwitted. I maintained that my brother's death had come as something of a shock, particularly as we had significant debts, and said I had heard that Vulliamy had occasionally lent money to people in the neighbourhood and asked directly whether he would consider extending me some credit.

"The man seemed to relax instantly and invited me to sit at a table in the centre of the room. He must have believed to that point that I had arranged the meeting to challenge him about the way he had treated Benjamin. With more than a hint of irony, I indicated that I would be forever indebted to him and had brought the Scotch as a goodwill gesture.

"Just imagine that, gentlemen! I'm in the lion's den and yet I have become the hunter - my greedy prey happy to distribute the whisky glasses and drink a toast or two to our financial transaction. So greedy were they that they didn't even realise I wasn't drinking with them. I watched as all three downed the first glass and Vulliamy poured a second. It was only on the third glass that the bottle stayed on the table. Serang was the first to fall, landing heavily on the floor and clutching his stomach. He began to be sick immediately.

Vulliamy never rose from his chair. His face turned ashen and within five minutes it was clear that he was dead. Bhandarry attempted to get up and make it to the kitchen. After only a few steps he slumped against the table, sending the whisky bottle and the glasses scattering across the floor.

"I sat and watched for twenty minutes, the only sound coming from Serang, who continued to lie on the floor. I guessed it would only be a short time before he too slipped away. I left the house and walked back to Louisa Street. I had the cart ready at the back gate and wheeled it the short distance to White Horse Lane. Using the rear door to Vulliamy's house, I first dragged his body to the cart, covered it with a tarpaulin and transported him to my home. His body went into the first of the three trenches I had already prepared and I quickly covered the corpse with soil. I then returned for Bhandarry Sayan.

"When I had buried the second body, I spent a short time indoors feeding Delilah and chipping away at the grave marker I had already begun to prepare for Vulliamy, believing that he deserved a Christian burial. But the light was beginning to fade and I was forced to abandon the task, returning once more to White Horse Lane.

"Entering the house for a third time, I knew instantly that something was amiss. As I entered the back door, Serang fell upon me, but in his weakened state I managed to fend him off, pushing him against a dresser. As he came at me again, I realised he had a gun in his hand and retreated back through the door, expecting to be shot any moment. I ran from the house, turning briefly to see Serang tripping over the abandoned cart. He seemed to be gaining in strength and as I ran out onto the Mile End Road could see that he was still following. In desperation I entered the *Bancroft Arms*. The rest you seem to know already..."

Christie slumped back in his chair. He looked visibly relieved as if recounting the tale had somehow lightened his burden. I made an observation in the sudden silence that had engulfed the room. "It is not unusual for antimony poisoning to affect people in different ways. Some, like Vulliamy, will decline very rapidly in the face of such toxicity. Serang was probably saved because he began to vomit straight away. This would have expelled the contents of his stomach immediately, the poison acting very much like its own antidote. Of course, it remains to be seen whether he will survive the ordeal. From what I hear, he is still very ill."

Christie shrugged. "What is done is done. I still cannot find it within me to feel any remorse. So, what will happen to me now, Mr Holmes?"

I could see there was no point in pretending that anything positive could ever come from the predicament that Christie now faced. Holmes clearly felt the same. "There is no easy way to say this, Mr Christie, but there seems little doubt that you will be tried and found guilty of murder. If you are willing to cooperate fully with the authorities and freely admit your guilt, there is some chance that your sentence might be commuted from one of execution to life imprisonment. That decision rests with you."

Christie did not seem perturbed by Holmes's words and had but one final request. "I know I am in no position to request anything further from either of you, but must ask. Would it be possibly for a decent home to be found for Delilah? I have a curious affection for that bird. She has been my only companion for some weeks now, and the only living creature I felt I could talk to throughout all of my troubles."

Holmes smiled at Christie and then turned to me with a sly wink. "Dr Watson and I understand completely. Rest assured

I will be pleased to look after the bird myself. Her conversation has already proved to be most enlightening."

It was about a week later when I next saw Holmes. I had arranged to meet him for lunch at the Grosvenor Hotel and arrived a few minutes early. To my surprise, he was already waiting in the reception area and as soon as I had entered the hotel he grasped me by the elbow and led me back out again to a waiting taxi.

"No time to waste, Watson. I'm afraid our luncheon will have to wait."

He bundled me into the back of the black cab and gave the driver our destination before continuing. "You might remember that at the start of the Christie case, I mentioned that I had been asked to investigate whether there might be a high-ranking officer within Scotland Yard who was taking bribes to protect Vulliamy. I feel confident that I will be able to reveal who that officer is in the next hour – a revelation likely to send shock-waves throughout the organisation."

I could not resist taunting him: "So this time we are looking for a mole, rather than a bird."

Holmes laughed out loud. "I've missed have your acerbic wit, Dr Watson." And with that, he slipped back into a short period of intense introspection, as only the great detective could. For the first time in over six years, it felt like a very joyous occasion indeed.

# About the Author

**Mark Mower** is a crime writer and historian whose passion for tales about Sherlock Holmes and Dr Watson began at the age of twelve, when he watched an early black and white film featuring the unrivalled screen pairing of Basil Rathbone and Nigel Bruce. Hastily seeking out the original stories of Sir Arthur Conan Doyle and continually searching for further film and television adaptations, his has been a lifelong obsession.

Now a member of the Crime Writers' Association and the Sherlock Holmes Society of London, Mark has written numerous books about true crime stories and fictional murder mysteries. He has contributed to a number of Holmes anthologies and his first volume of pastiches, *A Farewell to Baker Street* (MX Publishing) was published in December 2015. He is now working on a further volume of short stories.

# Copyright Information

# Also From Mark Mower

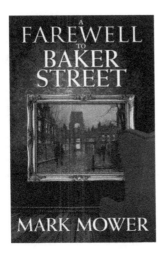

A Farewell To Baker Street

**An Affair of the Heart** demonstrates the critical interplay between the two men which made their partnership so memorable and endearing. **The Curious Matter of the Missing Pearmain** is a classic locked-room mystery, while **The Case of the Cuneiform Suicide Note** sees Dr Watson using his expert knowledge in helping to solve the mystery surrounding the death of an academic. **In A Study in Verse** the pair assists the Birmingham City Police in a complicated case of robbery which leads them towards a new and dangerous adversary. And to complete the collection, we have **The Trimingham Escapade**, the very last case the pair enjoyed together, which neatly showcases the inestimable talents of Sherlock Holmes. All of these tales are designed to contribute in some small part to the lasting memory of two extraordinary men who once occupied that setting we have come to know and love as 221B Baker Street.

# Also from MX Publishing

MX Publishing is the world's largest specialist Sherlock Holmes publisher, with over a hundred titles and fifty authors creating the latest in Sherlock Holmes fiction and non-fiction.

From traditional short stories and novels to travel guides and quiz books, MX Publishing cater for all Holmes fans.

The collection includes leading titles such as _Benedict Cumberbatch In Transition_ and _The Norwood Author_ which won the 2011 Howlett Award (Sherlock Holmes Book of the Year).

MX Publishing also has one of the largest communities of Holmes fans on Facebook with regular contributions from dozens of authors.

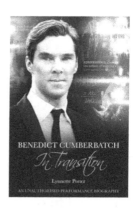

www.mxpublishing.com

# Also from MX Publishing

  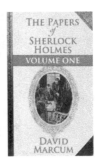

Our bestselling books are our short story collections;

'Lost Stories of Sherlock Holmes' , 'The Outstanding Mysteries of Sherlock Holmes', The Papers of Sherlock Holmes Volume 1 and 2, 'Untold Adventures of Sherlock Holmes' (and the sequel 'Studies in Legacy) and 'Sherlock Holmes in Pursuit', 'The Cotswold Werewolf and Other Stories of Sherlock Holmes' – and many more......

  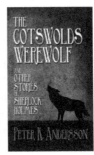

www.mxpublishing.com

# Also from MX Publishing

"Phil Growick's, 'The Secret Journal of Dr Watson', is an adventure which takes place in the latter part of Holmes and Watson's lives. They are entrusted by HM Government (although not officially) and the King no less to undertake a rescue mission to save the Romanovs, Russia's Royal family from a grisly end at the hand of the Bolsheviks. There is a wealth of detail in the story but not so much as would detract us from the enjoyment of the story. Espionage, counter-espionage, the ace of spies himself, double-agents, double-crossers...all these flit across the pages in a realistic and exciting way. All the characters are extremely well-drawn and Mr Growick, most importantly, does not falter with a very good ear for Holmesian dialogue indeed. Highly recommended. A five-star effort."
**The Baker Street Society**

www.mxpublishing.com

# Also from MX Publishing

## The Missing Authors Series

Sherlock Holmes and The Adventure of The Grinning Cat
Sherlock Holmes and The Nautilus Adventure
Sherlock Holmes and The Round Table Adventure

"Joseph Svec, III is brilliant in entwining two endearing and enduring classics of literature, blending the factual with the fantastical; the playful with the pensive; and the mischievous with the mysterious. We shall, all of us young and old, benefit with a cup of tea, a tranquil afternoon, and a copy of Sherlock Holmes, The Adventure of the Grinning Cat."
**Amador County Holmes Hounds Sherlockian Society**

www.mxpublishing.com

# Also from MX Publishing

## The American Literati Series

 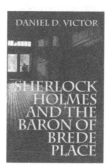 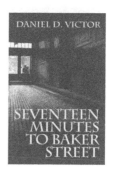

The Final Page of Baker Street
The Baron of Brede Place
Seventeen Minutes To Baker Street

"The really amazing thing about this book is the author's ability to call up the 'essence' of both the Baker Street 'digs' of Holmes and Watson as well as that of the 'mean streets' of Marlowe's Los Angeles. Although none of the action takes place in either place, Holmes and Watson share a sense of camaraderie and self-confidence in facing threats and problems that also pervades many of the later tales in the Canon. Following their conversations and banter is a return to Edwardian England and its certainties and hope for the future. This is definitely the world before The Great War."
**Philip K Jones**

www.mxpublishing.com

# Also from MX Publishing

## The Detective and The Woman Series

 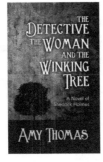 

The Detective and The Woman
The Detective, The Woman and The Winking Tree
The Detective, The Woman and The Silent Hive

"The book is entertaining, puzzling and a lot of fun. I believe the author has hit on the only type of long-term relationship possible for Sherlock Holmes and Irene Adler. The details of the narrative only add force to the romantic defects we expect in both of them and their growth and development are truly marvelous to watch. This is not a love story. Instead, it is a coming-of-age tale starring two of our favorite characters."
**Philip K Jones**

www.mxpublishing.com

# Also from MX Publishing

## The Sherlock Holmes and Enoch Hale Series

978 178092 7637

978178 092 4014

The Amateur Executioner
The Poisoned Penman
The Egyptian Curse


"The Amateur Executioner: Enoch Hale Meets Sherlock Holmes", the first collaboration between Dan Andriacco and Kieran McMullen, concerns the possibility of a Fenian attack in London. Hale, a native Bostonian, is a reporter for London's Central News Syndicate - where, in 1920, Horace Harker is still a familiar figure, though far from revered. "The Amateur Executioner" takes us into an ambiguous and murky world where right and wrong aren't always distinguishable. I look forward to reading more about Enoch Hale."
**Sherlock Holmes Society of London**

www.mxpublishing.com

CPSIA information can be obtained
at www.ICGtesting.com
Printed in the USA
FSHW021301100321
79368FS

9 781787 051201